Merrydown's Story

The Dragon-Master Trilogy

Book One

By

Nala ha'Levi

First published in Great Britain in 2016 by Nala ha'Levi

Formatted by The Amethyst Angel

Cover illustration by madappledesigns

ISBN: 978-1514145081

First Edition

Acknowledgements

I would like to thank my friends, Heather and Paul, the owners of a rather delightful establishment in Brighton called the Black Mocha, for their friendship and conversation, and for facilitating the meeting that led to the publishing of this book.

Many thanks to Michelle of The Amethyst Angel, for all the wonderful conversations about dragons and angels and for her editing and publishing help. She has brought my dream to life with her magic touch.

I'd also like to thank Liz of madappledesigns for creating the cover for this book, I appreciate your graphics wizardry!

This book is dedicated to all those many
thousands whose experiences and dreams
have led them to the truth, either encountering
dragons in the past, or by overcoming their
own personal dragons in this day and age.

Chapter One
Coming-of-Age

English Oxford Dictionary - **dragon:** A mythical monster

"Try telling them that the dictionary is infallible!"

Nala ha'Levi

"I've never seen a real one," said the boy. They continued walking up the hill towards the high mountain slopes, and its steep cliffs, leaving their village of Newcastle Emlyn far behind. His father smiled at him.

"Back in my childhood, there were still stories told about dragons, scores of them. It was said that they were just mythical creatures that didn't exist, but the village Elders knew better. And so, we were sent from the village to seek them out, and eventually found their nest and eggs too, hidden in those caves," his father said, pointing high up in the cliff-face in the direction they were walking.

"We were ordered to smash them all, and they shattered just like they were made of glass. But being young, I thought that there would be no harm in secretly keeping just one piece for myself."

The boy looked at his father with suspicion, yet his eyes widened with excitement. He thought to himself that this was bound to be just another tall tale, like those his father often told around the fireside at home, when they had company. But he sensed that there was something about his father that was somehow different this time, just by the look on his face.

Then his father began to recite a poem slowly, in a rather solemn voice:

"Breathing flame,
last night she came,
and in the morning –
if she had only stayed,
and not left me sleeping,
I would not have heard
of her death,
which left me sorely weeping.
Brave St. George had slayed my love- for
fame,
and left me with struggling with an awful
mystery.
Sadly, few ever knew my dragon lover's name.
Why then is this Saint so revered in history?

Appearing to have been overcome at this point, his father paused, and then quickly wiped away the beginning of a tear before continuing:

Surely, my friends, she deserves some mark in time?
To leave her out – would really be a crime.
'This singular omission has left me with revenge's burning desire.
Her name was - and to me, always will be – 'Fire!' "

The last word, his father had spoken quite firmly, yet softly, and this had caused the boy's mouth to fall open. His father reached out and placed his hand under his son's chin to close it, smiling gently as he did so.

He then lifted his hand away, yet kept it raised in front of the boy's face, as if to stay the obvious question that was sure to burst from his son's lips. He mused for a moment, and then he spoke in the solemn voice once again.

"Now you've reached sixteen years of age, you have today shared the secrets relating to your village's traditions and heritage as part of your initiation into manhood. Think yourself greatly privileged."

"I also think, Merrydown," he continued. "That it is high time I entrusted yet one more secret to your care. An important and very private matter. I have purposely waited until this very day, because as a much younger child, I had not been so sure that you would be able to keep that waggling tongue of yours still for too long. Especially in such an important matter as this one." The boy shook his head.

"And I think it is about time that you called me by my given name – Gavin – instead of Father."

"Yes, Father - sorry, Gavin," said Merrydown, pleased that at long last, he would now be allowed to address his father in such a familiar way, and yet he would never be as presumptuous as to consider that he was his equal. The most he hoped for was to make his father proud of him.

They had stopped walking when the poem had begun, but now his father looked over his shoulder towards where the sun was slowly sinking in the west.

Gavin sighed, then spoke again.

"Remember that you have today taken a sacred oath to protect our village, no matter what the cost. Now - no more questions for a while. We must continue with our walk. We still have a fair way to go before nightfall. We must reach those uppermost caves whilst we can still see our way. It's quite a tricky climb, but it will be treacherous in the dark," he said, raising his hand high and pointing to the highest of the caves.

Gavin started walking with purposeful strides this time, and it was all that Merrydown could do to keep pace with him. They walked on in silence, and thus quickly reached the bottom of the cliff.

Gavin led the way, in what seemed to Merrydown to be a familiar course to his father, and as they rose, the quickened pace allowed them to remain on that part of the cliff-face still lit by the setting sun's rays. When they were finally at the uppermost cave opening, his father stopped, and once again looked back in the direction from which they had come, to make sure that they were not being followed. This was something he had continually done on each part of their journey that day.

Merrydown too had copied his father each time, not quite sure exactly why, but had not seen anything untoward.

Within a few short paces now, he was about to find out the reason why Gavin had been so cautious. What secret was he about to be shown, he wondered.

They stepped into the cave entrance, which opened into a very long tunnel, and after several twists and turns, they entered a huge cave. It was impossible not to see that the floor of the cave was strangely lit with tiny little lights scattered all over the floor's surface.

In fact, the glimmering light from them illuminated the cave sufficiently for Merrydown to see that almost the entire ceiling of the cave was festooned with stalactites of all different colours and sizes.

Underneath, were stalagmites, whose slow

journey, drip by drip, up to join with them had been successful in several cases, over what must have been many hundreds, if not thousands of years. This had the effect of transforming the cave into that of a well-built shrine, just like the chapel back in his village.

Gavin bent down and picked up one of the small stones that gave off the strange light, and held it out to show Merrydown in the palm of his hand.

"These must never leave the cave except under very special circumstances," he said, offering it to Merrydown, "and I, as the secret Dragon-Master, will now pass on to you, my son, exactly what these are. I suggest you listen very carefully indeed."

Merrydown nervously held out his right hand, and his father carefully transferred the object from his own hand to that of his son's. It nestled there in the palm of Merrydown's hand.

Gavin then took out from his pocket what looked for all the world like a strange long white curved tooth, wrapped at the blunt end in a strip of ancient mottled green leather.

He touched the glimmering stone carefully with a cutting motion using the edge of the tooth, which appeared to neatly separate the stone into two uneven parts, the smaller piece of which Gavin retained.

The stone had originally had the texture and appearance of having been sand-blasted or tumbled in a river when first placed in his hand, and had felt just like any other stone, cold to the touch. Now, however, it instantly started to tingle and heat up.

He almost dropped it in surprise. His father's hand beneath his own prevented this from happening, and when he opened his hand to see what had caused this change to occur, to his surprise he could almost see right through the cleaved stone, just as one would with a crystal.

Or rather, right into it, for there, inside the stone, was a tiny curled-up serpent-like creature, the likes of which he had never seen before.

It was encased in what looked like solid glass, and yet the stone also retained its tumbled white exterior, apart from where the slice had been removed.

Strangely, Merrydown instinctively knew that the creature was a tiny dragon, and he could see that it was breathing!

Yet this was impossible. Surely the stone was solid.

"This is what we call a 'Shardlet'," Gavin said, as he gently removed the item from Merrydown's grasp and carefully placed the two parts back together again.

It again returned to its original opaque appearance and even more strangely, back into one piece, and was carefully placed back on the floor of the cave.

Merrydown felt that he had just witnessed something quite magical.

"Sit down lad," said Gavin affectionately, pointing to a nearby huge rocky shape, which looked for all the world like a broken-off stalagmite, for that was what it was. But it was wide enough for at least two full grown men to sit upon it. Nearby, lay the massive top section, somehow snapped off cleanly, like a mere twig, as if by some massive force.

"Where you now sit is known as 'The Seat of Knowing' - as we who are privileged to be called Dragon-Masters have come to call this particular spot, and I will instruct you further, beginning with a history lesson."

Merrydown took a seat on the outcrop his father had pointed at, whilst Gavin took a seat on another smooth outcrop facing him. Now accustomed to the light, on the far side of the cave Merrydown could now see where the top section of that particular stalagmite lay, amongst large boulders and rubble.

Chapter Two

The History Lesson

"Long ago," began Gavin. "Perhaps as many as five thousand years, dragons were to be found in folklore and in the oral histories of many different countries and cultures all around the world.

"They were both feared and also revered at the same time. I'm not sure that they really deserved that bad reputation at all, and for this reason, I rather like the idea that dragons are now in our family's care, as they have now been for many, many generations." Gavin stood up and began to pace.

"I personally love the idea that dragons existed at all, and not just in the imagination of story-tellers who have perhaps painted an unfair picture of them. Not only are they beings that are truly beautiful and very real, but uniquely, the honour has fallen to our family to protect them with our lives if necessary, and ensure that their existence is kept a secret for as long as is possible." He stopped pacing and put his hand on Merrydown's shoulder.

"There may well come a day when dragons will be called upon just as they were in the past, only this time they might be remembered in a more kindly fashion.

"Remember carefully to what I am telling you, Merrydown, for I don't doubt that you too will also have the honour of telling your own child these facts in due time, as part of your spoken history. I said facts, for this is what they are." He settled back down opposite Merrydown to continue his lesson.

"For many years, dinosaur bones were thought to be dragon's bones, but this error has since been corrected. In fact, there have never been any discoveries of actual dragon bones on dry land and thus they were consigned to mythology. I will tell you the secret of just why this is." His voice dropped to nearly a whisper, and Merrydown leaned forward to hear the secret.

"Dragons always go into the oceans to die. Using the last reserves of strength left in their bodies, they miraculously have always managed to do this, no matter how mortally wounded they are. And then their entire bodies are simply absorbed into the waters of the seas by the salt in the oceans, leaving no trace to ever be found. Or so most people now believe."

Merrydown nodded, as what his father was saying certainly made sense.

"Haven't you ever wondered just why river water tastes pure when it comes down from the hills, and yet, once it reaches the oceans and becomes absorbed into the great mass of the seas, it will always tastes salty?

"It cannot become clear again until it evaporates and goes up into the sky to form clouds. When the clouds have grown in size and become too full of water, the clouds release the water and it falls again as rain.

"That's just one of the magical properties that the dragons have bequeathed to mankind. This might sound fanciful to the un-initiated. The only pure water that we know of, is that which falls as rain from the clouds onto the mountain-tops in winter and freezes. When it melts in the spring and runs free from its icy confines, only then is it really pure.

"That's why the polar ice-caps are fresh water even though they are floating in very deep salty water. The compacted snow and ice have collected at the far ends of the world, well away from the sun's heat, and that is where we have the world's most wonderful store of pure water.

"There are even tales that dragons used to drag the icebergs into hot areas around the world where water was needed, then the ice melted in the sunshine so that crops could be grown to feed everyone all around the globe." Gavin shook his head. "Sadly, changes in climate meant that they were not needed anymore, and so they were regrettably killed off by people who feared them. But maybe that's just another theory, as there are so many. However, that's enough of science for today, let me get back to the history lesson."

Gavin noticed Merrydown fidgeting uncomfortably, and his voice became serious. "Please play careful attention to what I'm telling you, for both you and I share something really quite unique. We don't just share the same birthday. Both you and I were born in the Year of the Dragon too, exactly thirty-six years apart. That's three times the twelve year cycle of the Chinese calendar. You were actually born on my thirty-sixth birthday, one week later than you were expected."

"As you know, your grandfather was also born on the same day, again in the Year of the Dragon, and because of this happy circumstance, we have been granted the gift of talking to dragons, particularly when we need to ask for their help. They will always respond to us, as long as we hold them safe in our family's collective memories, as we have done. It is another mystery of our mind's untold power, for we never need to use spoken words to communicate with them, as pure thought is enough." Gavin smiled when Merrydown's eyes lit up at the mention of communicating with dragons.

“As well as being celebrated in the Far East, they appear in our culture too, lad, as you have already learned in school. Why, the story of St. George and the Dragon, of course. That is why a dragon also appears on our National Flag too. But let’s not get side-tracked.

“I will tell you about a brave soldier named George and how this soldier became a Saint. It was by supposedly slaying a fearsome dragon, but more of that tale in a minute. More importantly, I need to tell you all about our own family’s involvement with dragons.” He paused for a moment, and took his billycan out of his rucksack and took a drink from it.

“You see, there was an ancient village in the East going too far back in history to be precise as to the exact date, and the story tells us that it was constantly being plagued by a most dangerous and very grumpy dragon. It had terrorised the people of that village for a long, long time, by catching and eating them when they went down to the river to get water.

“A brave soldier called George was bored of doing nothing but marching, marching, marching, without ever fighting any real battles anymore, as the Crusades were over, so he decided to do something really worthwhile, rather than return home.

“‘I know,’ he said, ‘I will go and slay all the

troublesome dragons I've heard so much about that I can find.' Well, he rode from village to village, town to town, but could he find any truth to the stories he had heard? No, not one! But just as he was going to give up the search and return home, he arrived at a walled town built near a slow-flowing river, whose banks were very wide indeed, and also very marshy. The town itself sat at the foot of some low mountains where quite a lot of caves had been carved by rainwater over many thousands of years, exactly like those here at home," he said, gesturing at their surroundings.

"And in one of those caves lived this really nasty dragon. No-one had ever dared to ask him his name, so he was simply given the nickname 'Galumphing Old Grump', because he terrorised the townsfolk by chasing after them in a galumphing fashion. He often caught up with the people he was chasing, and then he ate them!

"The town Mayor held a meeting, and it was decided that they would give the dragon a big fat lamb every week. This worked for a while, but the dragon soon got fed up with the same diet, and anyway, all the lambs he had been eating had given him terrible indigestion, and kept repeating on him, so he became even grumpier than before. In those days they didn't know about mint sauce, you see, for that helps to take away the fatty taste of lamb," he laughed.

"It appeared that the dragon thought that people,

being much bigger, must be much tastier too, and it was fun to chase them and eat them, so he left the last lamb they offered him, and started chasing the townsfolk once again. So they got even more fed up with his bad behaviour. Something else had to be done.

"Another meeting was held and it was decided that it would be fair to draw lots to see who would be sacrificed to the dragon. Everyone in the town was entered into the first 'Unlucky Draw'. Sadly, their 'Spring Princess', the fairest maiden in the town, was the unfortunate one whose name was on the losing ticket. Having been lucky enough to be chosen to be the prettiest girl in town, and with a great future in front of her, it was just her luck to then be picked out as the one to be offered to 'Galumphing Old Grump' the dragon for his dinner!"

Merrydown looked appalled at the idea, obviously thinking of his own sister, Emmeline.

"And so, the next day, the poor Spring Princess was chained to a post, the base of which had been sunk into the ground by a group of nervous soldiers, who were not at all happy to have been given that task. They kept nervously looking over their shoulders every time they heard the dragon's stomach rumbling somewhere in the marsh, so they knew he was there all right.

"The post had been placed near the marsh where the dragon usually hid during the daytime, just watching and waiting for his next victim to come along. The dragon's tummy could be heard rumbling even louder, and he began to stamp his clawed feet with hunger, and thrashing his scaly tail about, so they knew he was there. That made them very nervous indeed.

"The 'Spring Princess' – her name was Jasmin, I think – sobbed her heart out, thinking that this was her last day on Earth, when George came riding by. He quickly found out what was to befall her, and offered to fight the dragon – a worthy opponent at last.

"A terrible battle ensued, and although mortally wounded, George finally slew 'Old Grump'. The town Mayor started a petition which all the people signed, asking the Pope to make George a Saint, and that is what happened." Gavin pulled out a handkerchief and blew his nose before continuing.

"There have been similar stories like this all over the world, and aside from one exception, the dragon was always killed at the end of the battle, and the 'George' in the story always became a hero.

"In our story, however, the dragon wasn't killed outright, but was very badly wounded, and she cleverly pretended that she was dead. Our ancestors then secretly helped this female dragon - named *'Fire'* – to get down to the ocean, in order to allow her to swim out to sea, where she could then die. Before leaving, she told her rescuers about the eggs she had left in this very cave.

"They had to use a huge hay-cart pulled by four massive shire-horses, each over seventeen-hands high. Their hooves were covered with sacks so that they could not be heard when they went through the villages on their way to the sea, so no-one but our family knew what really happened to the dragon. It took a whole night to travel some ten miles from our village to the sea at Aberporth Bay."

Gavin noticed that Merrydown was beginning to look very sleepy. "I will tell you just one more story, another reason why dragons have such a bad reputation, then we will rest awhile."

"In China, dragons are celebrated at the beginning of each Year of the Dragon, when thin bamboo frames are fashioned into the shape of an open-mouthed dragon. These light frames are then covered in red and green tissue-paper, and candles lit inside them to allow them to float up into the air when released, as the air inside them is heated-up, giving them lift.

"Sadly, and inevitably, some catch fire if the candle-flame becomes too large, and they collapse in a ball of fire, with flames seeming to come from the very dragon's mouth.

"This has probably happened so often that sometimes the balls of fire fall onto a poor peasant's home which then catches alight, as that simple building might have been made of wood, covered with straw or reed-thatch to keep out the rain, just as some of our homes are still today. Thus, in folklore, a dragon's breath seemingly had really started the fire!"

Gavin paused and Merrydown saw his opportunity to speak.

"Tell me more about the dragon's eggs, Dad, um, I mean Gavin."

"Well, some poor souls have stumbled upon this cave by accident, and then run clear of the place - calling it enchanted, or even cursed - and yet strangely, only our family can enter it without fear, and recognise the dragon's eggs for what they really are - a piece of magical history. The instrument you saw me use to cut open the stone is, in fact, a genuine dragon's tooth. It is the only true relic of its kind left in the world. It has come from a real full-size dragon." Gavin patted his jacket pocket where the knife-like tooth was securely tucked away.

"In fact it was a gift to my predecessors from the dragon I spoke about with such reverence as we walked here. It was a gift given out of pure love, and was given to one of our long dead ancestors, for helping the fatally wounded *'Fire'* to reach the sea.

"She wouldn't have made it at all without the help our family gave her after St. George's lance pierced her side, and so, this particular dragon's tooth, is a priceless relic, which has always passed down from father to their eldest son or daughter on that special evening following their 'coming-of-age' ceremony."

Gavin sighed. "In case something terrible might befall you, your sister, Emmeline will also need to be told the story in a couple of years' time when she too, reaches sixteen years of age. But it is *you*, Merrydown, who is the first chosen one of your generation, as part of your birth-right, to be given the dragon's tooth today." Gavin pulled out the tooth and carefully handed it to Merrydown.

"This unique artefact I now entrust to you, Merrydown, for safe keeping, now that you have come of age and know of its existence. You must ensure to keep it well hidden at all times, for it has magical properties. It truly is an article like no other I know of.

"In the wrong hands it could wreak havoc, for it can be used to release all the dragons from inside each one of these stones, where they slumber, in the form of Shardlets," he said, gesturing to the twinkling stones on the cave floor.

"Whilst in the darkness of this cave, a Shardlet will always remain small enough to sleep happily in the palm of your hand inside the shard or egg, and will do so with no ill effect to either you or your sister.

"But, take one outside, and it will instantly and magically grow to full size in daylight in the blink of an eye. Before a connection is established, a full sized dragon is a dangerous creature who cannot be controlled. That is why we arrived here as night fell, to ensure that should you have run from here in fright at what you had been told, with that egg still grasped in your hand, we would have had an uncontrollable dragon on our hands. A huge dragon allowed to roam uncontrolled would cause untold rumours, and panic would then have spread like wildfire."

Chapter Three

Followed After All

Merrydown shivered as he tucked the dragon's tooth deep within the folds of his thick coat, and followed his father towards the tunnel that led to the cave entrance. Gavin didn't enter the tunnel however, but walked to an alcove to the left-hand side, where he proceeded to pull out enough kindling to build a fire.

It was obvious that they were going to stay there for the night, and this was the means by which they would keep warm. It was also obvious to Merrydown that a fire lit this far inside the cave would never be visible from outside, thanks to the many turns in the tunnel they had to first walk through, before entering the last dragon's cave itself.

Gavin also unpacked the rucksack he had been wearing over his shoulder, and took out some thick crusty sandwiches, wrapped in greaseproof paper, and also a large billy-can of tea. It was now obvious to Merrydown that an overnight stay was expected, and prepared for by Gavin, well in advance of this special day.

He soon had a good fire burning, and it wasn't long before they were tucking into their supper of hot tea and tasty cold chicken sandwiches with mustard.

They chatted briefly about nothing in particular, as Gavin could see that the youngster was worn out from the climb and all the new things he had learned earlier that day at his coming-of-age ceremony. Once finished eating and drinking, and finally warmed up once again, they both curled up by the fire, and, using their back-packs as pillows, were soon fast asleep.

After what seemed like no time at all, Merrydown woke to find Gavin already up and the fire burning steadily, with the hot water almost ready to make tea again. Gavin had obviously been awake for some time.

He put his finger quickly up to his lips, in a 'Shush' motion, to stop Merrydown speaking.

Gavin moved over to Merrydown and pointing at a motionless figure on the floor, he whispered in his ear. "Despite all my precautions, we were followed. When that fellow over there comes to, you must be very guarded in what you say in front of him." He continued whispering. "It seems that he must have bumped his head rather badly on an outcrop of rock on the tunnel ceiling." He winked and pointed to his tea flask, which now had a big dent in it.

"He was very sly, following us up the mountain like that last night without us spotting him. But after a night spent sleeping out in the cold night air, he certainly didn't have his wits about him this morning. I heard him coming long before he entered the tunnel, as I was awake very early, long before he had stirred, and was waiting for him when he stumbled into the tunnel. That billy-can still had plenty of water in it and was quite heavy!" He chuckled quietly.

"Anyway, when he wakes up and asks questions, we will tell him that we simply came up here to watch the sun set last night on your life as a child, and also to mark the dawn of a new time in your life once the sun rose again. I had done exactly this with my father many years ago when I became of age too.

"We simply took shelter in this cave that we had stumbled upon by happy circumstance, nothing more. There are always lots of caves on these mountains that shepherds use for shelter at night."

He winked again, and moved back to where he had been sitting, and just in time too.

The crumpled figure on the ground in the far corner of the cave entrance started moving and both father and son had smiles on their faces as they heard a loud groaning coming from the man.

He slowly sat up and turned towards them, and

the reflection of the fire's glow twinkled in his eyes, making them look quite devilish and scary to Merrydown.

The man was certainly not from their village, nor from those around the nearby villages who had turned up for yesterday's ceremony. He was, therefore, a complete stranger to them both, and therefore Gavin's concern became even greater.

He stood up shakily, rubbing the obvious bump on the side of his head, wincing at its tenderness. He staggered over to them both, at which Gavin stood up in order to protect them both should it be necessary.

The man was quite thin, and was wearing a long coat that looked more like a cloak to Merrydown. A string of questions flew from the man's lips as he steadied himself, and sat down on the rocky outcrop that Gavin had been sitting on the previous night. He looked cautiously at the ceiling of the cave above his head as he sat.

"How did I get here? Who are you? How did I get this lump on my head?" Without waiting for a reply, he began to introduce himself. "I'm a writer and I'm just visiting the area and recording the folklore stories in order to complete my latest book," he said. "My name is Richard Conman. You might have heard of me."

Father and son both shook their heads. It sounded like a plausible explanation, but why on earth would he be doing that almost at the top of *their* mountain and at night-time too? Very mysterious indeed.

They both looked at each other with raised eyebrows, which broke the tension in the air.

"I'm Gavin, and this is my son Merrydown. Yes, I know it's an unusual name, but it has been in our family for generations, and it was his grandfather's name, and his grandfather's before him too."

He stopped, realising he had probably said far too much, as even that information might possibly make the stranger hang around the area, and neither of them wanted that. They were both aware that there was so much more to discuss about what Merrydown had been shown last night, so the last thing they wanted was for this stranger to latch on to them.

Gavin also didn't want to seem too unfriendly, and decided to answer the man's first question and then hurry him on his way.

"I found you in the tunnel leading into this cave when we came here to make a cup of hot tea, as I knew that shepherds kept dry timber here for just such a purpose. You must have bumped your head on a low bit of the roof in the darkness of the tunnel, and knocked yourself out cold.

"When you finally came to, had you wandered even further into the cave, and got lost in one of the many tunnels inside here, you may never have been found. It's lucky for you that we found you when we came up here to watch the sunrise. I didn't think that your injury was serious enough to call out a rescue team, and so we have simply waited for you to wake up."

The stranger nodded slowly.

"Are you feeling better now? Do you want a mug of tea?" Gavin felt he had said enough for the present, and would wait to see what else the stranger would have to say that might explain why he was really up 'their' mountain.

It was obvious that neither father nor son were really happy with his explanation so far.

Chapter Four

Challenging Myths

Richard Conman sat by the fire, warming himself and drinking tea from a mug that Gavin had poured out for him from the billy-can, oblivious to the fact that it was this very vessel that had knocked him out and caused him to suffer the lump on his head. He now believed that he really had bumped his head on a protruding rock in the tunnel.

He spoke again, hoping to fool this father and son, little knowing that he was about to condemn himself with another lie.

"I'm staying in the village, but decided to go for a walk, and I got myself totally lost in the darkness. So I continued on up the mountain in order to get my bearings from a higher viewpoint, and that's when I saw the light from your fire back down the tunnel."

What he didn't realise, was that both Gavin and Merrydown knew that this was impossible. There were so many turns in the tunnel leading into the cave itself that the light from the fire would never be seen from outside!

Richard noticed, that they both seemed to be a little guarded now, and was confused when Gavin turned to him and smiled.

"Well now," he said. "Once you have finished drinking your tea, we'll gather up our bits and pieces and make our back down to our little village.

"Both Merrydown and I have both already enjoyed watching quite a lovely sun-rise, and will now have quite a lot to do today once we get back home."

Richard sensed that he was being dismissed, and rubbed his head again which was aching.

"Anyway, it would seem that you are not suffering anything worse that a bad bump on the head. I guess that you will have a bit of a headache for a day or two, but now that you have come to and are sitting up fine, no doubt you will be on your way, as the sun has been up for some time. It's a fine day, so you will find your way back easily I'm sure."

Richard could only nod in agreement. He was hoping to be able to convince this duo of what he mistakenly considered were a couple of country-bumpkins into agreeing to walk him back down to the village of Newcastle Emlyn, from where he had first followed them from the evening before.

He slowly stood up, and flicked the last dregs of

his tea from his mug into the dying fire, and he handed the empty mug to Gavin with a quick nod of thanks. Then he walked over to the far side of the cave, to where he had been placed, unconscious, by Gavin a couple of hours before. He bent down and picked up his coat and pack from where he had been laying, as Gavin and Merrydown both picked up burning branches from the fire to light their way out of the cave.

"I'm ready, and I would appreciate it if you kind chaps will show me how to get out of here. I'm sure you are right, I probably would have never been able to work out which way to go." He paused, as father and son moved carefully around the far edge of the cave, purposely going the long way round and past several natural openings in the rock that could have led anywhere, as if to emphasise how difficult it would have been for him to find his way out of the cave, had he been alone.

They finally exited the cave slowly through the long tunnel. Yawning to himself, as he hadn't quite fully recovered, and gingerly rubbing the lump on his head, Richard sat down slowly on a boulder at the cave-mouth.

"Give me a minute please, will you, I'm still feeling a bit wobbly." He pointed to Gavin's back. "Have you any water left in your backpack please?'

Gavin stopped and turned slowly. He removed

his backpack and took out the dented article and shook it to see how much water was left, then offered it to him.

Richard gratefully took the offered can from Gavin and took a very long drink, finishing the last of the water entirely. He then handed it back and said, “Sorry, but I’ve finished the water off. When we get back down to your village, I must buy you a new one of those, as a way of saying thanks for your help. This one is quite battered and dented, and has certainly seen quite a heavy use in its time, I guess.”

Both Gavin, and Merrydown too, appeared to be on the verge of laughter at his last comment, and whilst Gavin stowed the battered old billy-can back into his backpack, he replied, “It most certainly has!”

They all readied themselves to move back down to the village. And despite feeling unwelcome, Richard walked alongside them, hoping to accompany them all the way back to the village.

There was little opportunity of holding much of a conversation on the way down, as Gavin led the way, and Merrydown followed on behind Richard.

When at last they finally reached the village, Richard felt and looked totally worn out, and certainly needed a bath, due to the many slips he had suffered on the climb down, due to being less nimble than either of his guides.

They, on the other hand, looked quite fresh,

obviously quite used to the hard country life. Gavin pointed to the village inn and said, "I'm afraid this is where we part company, Richard, but as you look worn out, I'm sure you'll rest well in your room for tonight and have a wash and tidy-up before moving on."

"Oh, I guess we will meet quite soon," Richard replied. "As I expect I'll stick around for a few days to collect more information for my book."

Looking less than pleased at this, the pair then turned and walked away from him before he could say anything else. He was still standing outside the inn, exactly where they had left him, openly watching where they were headed.

They both waved a brief goodbye as they turned their heads on reaching the crossroads at the centre of the village, and then disappeared from sight around the corner, seemingly heading for home.

Aching and weary, Richard headed to the inn, hoping for a nice hot bath to mull over what had just transpired.

Chapter Five

Looming Threat

Easter was usually a special time in the village, and despite the rationing in effect, Merrydown over-indulged in the eating of all the Easter eggs friends and family had given him.

His coming-of-age celebrations had only taken place a couple of weeks before, and afterwards his apprenticeship with his father continued as normal, whatever normal was, because nothing would ever be the same again. For now, Merrydown had a secret.

He had planned to enjoy the Easter holiday as much as he was still allowed, though he wished he could still sing with the male voice choir, but as his voice had got a little more grown-up and growly sounding, he was no longer able to. But that was the least of his concerns.

He tried to remain cheerful, despite everyone talking about the War with the Germans which had begun following their invasion of Poland on the first day of September the previous year, in 1939.

The mood was starting to spoil the holiday feeling for everyone, because no-one had forgotten how badly the First World War had affected their world.

Not one family in the village had escaped the horrors of losing someone who had gone off to fight and never returned, so nothing would ever be the same for the whole village.

After his return from that first visit to the cave in the hills, Merrydown had carefully hidden the dragon's tooth knife amongst his clothes in the chest of drawers in his room. He looked at it in wonder every day, whilst checking that it was still safely hidden away.

He was itching to go back to see that magical cave once again with his father, and to learn more about his responsibilities now that he was a Dragon-Master, for he had been told by Gavin that it was only in the cave that secrets would be passed on.

This holiday period would be just about the most perfect time that they could both arrange to make a visit for a few hours under the pretence of hunting for rabbits and not be missed by anyone.

And so, once food and drink were arranged in the morning, they set off for the hills, again, taking care not to be followed. To his great surprise, this time, Merrydown was being allowed to lead the way. He supposed it was because he was now carrying the dragon's tooth knife well hidden inside his clothes, where he could feel it tingling against his body.

It was in fact to ensure to Gavin that his son could remember the way by himself should he need to do so.

There was still a light dusting of hoar-frost on the grass, which made a crunching sound underfoot as they walked, evidence of how cold it had been night before.

The air was still cold enough to cause both Merrydown's and Gavin's breath to give the impression that they were both smoking, which of course neither of them had ever done.

At the foot of the cliff where the cave was hidden, and roughly half-way along the route itself, Merrydown faltered, not knowing which was the best path to take, and so Gavin decided to take the lead, with a quick dig in Merrydown's ribs as he passed him.

"It really is important that you try and memorise the route, in case you have to make the journey when I'm not with you for any reason, should you ever need to enlist the aid of a real dragon to help our village," Gavin said. "And it is you, Merrydown, who will be the one to undertake the initiation of your sister instead of me when she turns sixteen, so it will be your duty to lead her up to that cave." He pointed up the cliff-face.

"You will then need to tell her all about the mysteries and secrets surrounding our family's special connection with dragons, and our responsibility of caring for the safety of the Shardlets, and their secret location within that cave.

"Do remember also that Emmeline will not be able to become a Dragon-Master herself, as she was not born in the Year of the Dragon, but instead, she will be gifted with other special powers as a member of our family, of which I will tell you more once we reach the safety of the cave. Now follow me, lad and do try and remember the way." He wagged his forefinger at Merrydown, but his face and smile showed that he was not cross.

"The way was certainly difficult for me to remember too, the first time my father showed it to me, and the weather has definitely worn away all the secret markings that I made in the cliff-face all those years ago."

On finally reaching the safety of the cave entrance once again, Gavin allowed Merrydown to lead them through the tunnel with the help of the flaming branch Gavin had handed to him, and they both entered the cave where the Shardlets lay untouched and twinkling.

Merrydown automatically took his place on the 'Seat of Knowing' while Gavin remained standing and began to reveal more about the cave and the secrets of being a Dragon-Master to his son.

"This cave itself has some magical properties

that I'm still learning about, and I've been a Dragon-Master since I turned sixteen and was given the dragon's tooth knife by my father, just as I have now passed it down to you."

"The first of these magical properties," he warned, "is the fact that, as this is the last-known place where the dragon named *'Fire'* created her nesting site; the labyrinth of tunnels within this cave have a magical way of moving around. So a stranger, entering the cave by one of the four entrance tunnels that still exist, could be stumbling around in the semi-darkness for days and never ever find his way out." Gavin smiled. "Why, like we told our 'friend' Richard a couple of weeks ago, he would have ended up dying of thirst and hunger, as did so many in the past. This is why shrivelled-up corpses appear in paintings of dragons in our local library. But you and I, Merrydown, as the current keepers of the dragon's-tooth relic you brought with you, both have special protection, and so that danger is removed.

"The Shardlets are kept small and twinkling by the magnetic properties of the rock from which this place was formed millennia ago. But if taken outside the cave, the Shardlets instantly become normal sized dragons eggs, which are huge, and it would take a very strong man indeed to roll one back into the cave again. Even together, we certainly wouldn't be up to the task, I fear."

He paused to allow Merrydown to absorb what he was being told. Gavin then began listing all of the unique magical properties that he was aware of, that dragons could call upon if needed, but only to help mankind in times of deep trouble.

He already knew that from his first visit what would happen if they were ever to be taken out of the safety of their secret hiding place within the cave system by a stranger.

"These little Shardlets," Gavin said, pointing whilst moving over to where the twinkling crystal stones lay, and picking one up. "When released from their crystal cocoons with the help of the dragon's-tooth knife you now have in your safe keeping, will sit happily in the palm of your hand just like a pet mouse. But, as I mentioned before, taken out into the daylight, they will become full-sized, and very real dragons in the blink of an eye.

"They can take a very deep breath, which makes them even larger, and then, mysteriously, they can actually fly if required to do so, despite the fact they do not have wings. They just think 'UP!' and up they can fly, using their tails to steer."

Merrydown blinked in amazement and wondered why the dragon on their flag had wings.

"The peasants who drew dragons in the past, may have seen them flying, and assumed that they did so by flapping their incorrectly imagined and non-existent wings. It wasn't easy for anyone in the past to give a true description of a dragon simply because most of the people who had seen one would be running away in fear of their lives!

"Dragons also have a magical power to make both themselves and their rider become invisible, as long as the rider remains in contact with the dragon.

"The Dragon-Rider's seat is as strong as the dragons' scales, and thus, in the past, arrows and spears simply bounced off, should they have been attacked by human beings, who are their most feared adversary.

"A dragon had just one large vulnerable area, which was on its underbelly, which is why dragons wore armour made of additional scales which they grew especially for the purpose. If any were damaged, they were like a shark's tooth, and when they fell off, they were quickly replaced by new ones in no time at all. This left only its mouth, which, when open, might allow a sword or something similar to pierce deep down a dragon's throat. This was why a dragon had such a fearsome array of teeth, for they could quickly close and deflect such a weapon."

Merrydown blinked at the amount of information his father had just imparted, and did his best to concentrate.

"Remember, they didn't breathe fire. That really was a myth, but it was one that they were keen to perpetuate. What most people didn't know, was that uniquely, all dragons could also think as one unit when necessary and they also shared memories, so it was no surprise to be told that since the terrible incident with St. George, all dragons, and that included the Shardlets too, knew how important it was to stay hidden out of sight, in order to protect themselves properly."

"Gosh!" exclaimed Merrydown, after Gavin had stopped talking. "That's an awful lot of things for me to remember."

"Yes," agreed Gavin, finally taking the chance to sit down, after having paced up and down whilst talking. "But your dragon will expect you to remember all of them, and give him a fitting name to answer to, when you first release him, if that ever happens."

"That's a huge responsibility," was all Merrydown could say, shaking his head in wonder at all that he had been told.

Once he had repeated all that Gavin had told him correctly, and rehearsed them within the privacy of the cave, and his father was happy with his rendition of the poem about the dragon named *'Fire'* without too many mistakes, it was time for them to climb carefully back down the mountain and head for home.

As they neared the village inn, who should they chance to bump into, but that strange character Richard Conman. Much to their surprise he was either still around after two weeks, or for some reason he had come back again.

“Hello,” he said, greeting them with what could best be described as a sort of half-smile. “Nice to see you both again. Funny time to watch either a sunrise or sunset though. I saw you coming back from the mountains, and would love a chat with you. You see, I’ve already exhausted all the villagers with my continuing quest for any folklore tales, but so far, I haven’t got any of yours, even though your family happens to have been living in Newcastle Emlyn longer than anyone else.”

It was now so very obvious to both of them that this Mr Conman had been snooping about, and asking far too many questions for their liking. He made a great show of looking at his wristwatch.

“As it’s now tea-time, perhaps you chaps will be kind enough to stand me a cup of tea? I’ll walk back with you now, as I know it’s not far to your home?”

They became even more wary of him now that it was clear that he had been waiting to stop the pair of them as they headed for home. They were caught on the spot, and felt that they weren’t really in any position to refuse, as they didn’t want to appear unfriendly.

When they eventually got to their house, and the tea was brewing nicely in their best teapot, both they and Richard sat themselves down. With a quick signal of his finger against his nose, and unseen by their visitor, Gavin had already ensured that Merrydown did not speak. There was an ominous silence for a while, and then, just when Gavin was about to speak, Richard spoke first.

"I haven't been exactly honest with either of you about who I really am," he said. "But I had to be very careful to find the right people to talk to, and so I have been using my cover-story of collecting folklore tales in order to conceal what I was really doing here in Wales."

Merrydown looked at his Dad, their suspicions were being confirmed.

"I really work for British Intelligence, and as this awful war with Germany doesn't appear to have an end in sight, London thinks that you may be able to help your country's war effort. Strange rumours have reached London that you could well have the means to help us defeat Mr. Hitler and his cronies."

He then showed them some really tatty-looking and smudged ID papers, supposedly from the War Office, to prove who he was, but because of their sad state, both Gavin and Merrydown were still very wary, and gave nothing away.

Chapter Six

Uncertain Futures

"I'm really sorry," said Gavin, "but I'm not sure what you are referring to."

Shaking his head in disbelief, Mr Conman said, "Oh, come now, everyone in the village says that you can call up dragons. That's why you don't have a house in the village itself, because the rest of the villagers have always been scared that your dragons would set the whole village alight when they come and visit you. Your family, and their contact with dragons, is all the villagers seemed talk about when given a drink or two and half a chance."

Gavin laughed out loud. "Surely you don't believe that rubbish," he said, hoping to throw their visitor off the scent, and try to get rid of him once and for all. "That really is all it is, just folklore. Just because our house is one of the oldest ones in the village, and was one of the first ones to be built of stone rather than wood, wattle and daub, doesn't mean that we have anything to do with dragons. Some of the villagers around here are very superstitious, and terrible gossips too," he said, trying to make light of the situation. "It's these characters that keep our communities alive, especially if a stranger has been buying them a few beers. But that's all it is, just a tale, nothing more. Now, drink up your tea or it will go cold."

It surprised them both when he refused a second cup of tea, when this was offered to him.

Gavin hoped he had now said enough to put his visitor off, and perhaps finally put an end to his poking around. Maybe he would soon be on his way back to London, if that is where he really was from. Gavin already had his doubts.

Once they had chatted briefly about the weather, and how the war was going, Mr Conman made his excuses and left, just as they were pouring themselves a third cup of tea.

"Strange that he isn't a tea drinker," said Merrydown, shortly after Mr Conman left.

"That's exactly what I was thinking," said Gavin. "So I'm going to get up early in the morning and go down to the telephone-box in the village. I'll make a call to my old army captain in London. He works for the War Office now you know, and will be sure to check this chap Conman out, if to do nothing more than put my mind at rest. I'm no expert, but the papers he showed me looked very suspicious indeed, because they were so tatty-looking. It's not only that, but fancy refusing a second cup of tea, it's just not British!"

"We'd better keep an eye on him until he's been checked out then," said Merrydown softly, almost to himself, knowing that that would be easy to do without raising any suspicions, as it was still the Easter holiday time.

With that, they both prepared supper together as a surprise for Mum and Emmeline, who were, like most women in the village, busy working on the local farms to help with the war effort, by keeping food production going. Merrydown worked with his father Gavin in their carpentry workshop adjacent to their home, which was situated just on the outskirts of the village.

For his own peace of mind, after a restless night, the first thing the next day, even before he had opened his workshop, Gavin did make that call to Captain Greaves in London, using the red telephone-box next to the village green.

And so, after putting two penny coins into the money slot provided, Gavin made the call to London. He was then told to hang up the telephone and wait until they could find Captain Greaves, and he would ring back shortly.

Gavin knew that this was normal procedure to ensure that he really was making the call from Wales, as the call would have to be routed through the telephone operator, and would, without doubt, be monitored. After all, this was wartime, and one couldn't be too careful.

A few minutes later the telephone rang, and the operator said that she had found the Captain, and he was just making his way back to his office, and would Gavin please keep the line open and wait to speak to him.

"Hello Gav, Old Bean!" Gavin was delighted to hear his old army captain's gruff voice at the other end of the line calling him by his nickname once again. "How's things going out in the sticks? What's this call all about then? And how can I help?" Typically, always a barrage of questions, and so he quickly explained the situation to his old army boss about his concerns regarding Richard Conman.

When he was through, Captain Greaves asked him to hold on again whilst he made a couple of calls on his other telephone, and placed that receiver onto his desk, so Gavin could hear the other conversation. It was obvious that he was talking to someone very senior in Intelligence

When he heard the Captain say, "What?", "Good Lord!" and "Yes, he's still on the other line, just wait while I ask him." His mind was already racing ahead. *What on earth could the problem be?* he wondered.

Captain Greaves' voice again came on the line.

"What colour was the printing on this chappie's papers, my colleague wants to know, and what colour hair does he have?"

"Why, it was faded blue ink, and his hair was a sort of dirty-blond colour and longish too," said Gavin.

"Are you certain?" came the response.

After a brief moments' thought, he said: "Yes, definitely to both."

This was relayed back to whoever Captain Greaves was talking to, and then he heard the captain's voice once again.

"Apparently we have a huge problem, Gav. The Ministry of Defence never use blue ink on ID, only black, and our chap with that name hasn't reported back for duty for a couple of weeks, which is most weird. We've already had this flagged this up by his Control, who raised the alarm. They have also had a chap call at his address several times, in case he had gone under deep cover for any reason, but without any luck."

Before Gavin could respond, the captain continued.

"Oh, and our man is practically bald. Has been since he was in his early twenties, just like his father. You did well to be suspicious, your chap is probably a spy working for the Germans. I just hope that they are holding our Richard Conman alive and well somewhere, and haven't bumped him off!"

Gavin was then asked to very discreetly keep an eye on the imposter without raising his suspicions, until Captain Greaves' colleague in Intelligence could get a specialised team to Wales and observe him for a day or two before arresting him. In this way, it was hoped that he might lead them to anyone else working for the enemy too.

"Tell no-one about this," he was warned. "As it's very hush hush, indeed!"

Gavin was then read the Official Secrets Act over the telephone by Captain Greaves, and now, Gavin felt like a real Spy!

He did, however, persuade them to agree to Merrydown being told, as they could then cover the day and night watches in turn, with Gavin covering the night watch himself, until the promised team arrived from London.

Gavin and Merrydown cleared away the breakfast things once the girls had gone off to work. Before they opened the workshop, Gavin suggested that they both stretched their legs before moving some of the logs needed for the fire, nearer to the house. What he really wanted to do however, was to ensure they weren't overheard whilst he told Merrydown about the call to London.

When Gavin told Merrydown what had transpired, he looked seriously concerned, but then he suddenly smiled and as he turned to his father, he said. "I've been thinking, and have just come up with a strange idea that may solve our surveillance problems, and I hope you'll agree. There is someone else who can help us keep an eye on that imposter without ever being seen. Then we could then carry on business in the workshop as normal."

Gavin didn't want to go against the advice of Captain Greaves, but was still very keen to hear what Merrydown's suggestion would be.

Chapter Seven

The Awakening

They continued to move the logs and lay them in neat piles, until there was a good selection right next to the back door of the house, in readiness for making a lovely fire in the hearth.

This made it easier to find the different-sized logs necessary to build up a decent fire quickly in the dark at night without needing to leave a light on, which wasn't allowed. This was because a light could easily be seen from above, and that would give the enemy planes a target to drop their bombs onto. After all, this was war-time, and everyone kept their curtains tightly drawn together at night.

"Right then, Merrydown, tell me what this great idea is that you have in mind then. I'm really keen to know how we can keep watch on our Mr Conman whilst we are both in the workshop. It seems to me that it's impossible to be in two places at the same time," Gavin said, once he had made sure no-one else was around.

Merrydown then told Gavin what he had

suddenly thought of, which caught his father quite off-guard.

"I remembered what you told me about the dragons, and a weird thought suddenly came into my head."

"Go on," said Gavin, smiling at his son. "I'm all ears."

"I don't know why, but suddenly I imagined that I was back in the cave again, and I was holding that Shardlet in my hand, and calmly walking out of the cave in broad daylight, but I didn't know why. Then I remembered you had told me that dragons have the ability to become invisible. Why can't we ask one of them to help us keep a watch on Mr. Conman?"

"That's an interesting idea, Son, but it could be very dangerous," said Gavin.

"Not if I have a connection with the Shardlet. Didn't you say that we would be able to communicate with each other?"

"Yes I did." Gavin was thoughtful for a moment. "When you held the Shardlet in the cave, did you by any chance have a name in your head when you held it?"

"Why, yes, I did," said Merrydown. "I remembered the story you told me and also the poem you recited about the dragon called '*Fire*', and I called him – strangely, I somehow knew it was a male Shardlet – and I heard the words – '*Son-of-Fire.*'"

"Ah!" sighed Gavin. "That explains it. The Shardlet must have instantly bonded with you, and perhaps he sensed that you may need his help. Now all you have to do is to find that particular 'stone' again, and then we can enlist your dragon's help to secretly keep an eye on the spy by using his remarkable gift of invisibility."

Merrydown looked pleased that his father liked his idea.

"I hope your memory is sharp. Do you think that you can find your way back up to the cave alone, and not only that, but also find that same Shardlet, whilst I keep watch back here?"

"I think so," replied Merrydown. "I can almost feel him calling to me inside my head whilst we are talking together. I'll just need to go and fetch the dragon's tooth knife from my room in order to be able to release him. If I do get stuck inside the cave, I'm sure that Son-of-Fire will instinctively know the right way out."

* * *

Merrydown bade Gavin farewell and made his way out of their gate. He then went down through the village and walked back up to the cave, remembering to check several times en-route that he was not being followed by anyone.

Gavin's last words of advice were still going around in his head, and he wondered how on earth

Gavin knew all these things. It occurred to him that Gavin must have had to enlist a dragon's help at some time in the past, but until now, had never spoken about this to his son.

"Remember to stand well back when you take that first step into daylight from the tunnel," he had warned Merrydown. "As your dragon will grow to full-size in the blink of an eye. Then you must wait a short while more, until he has gained control of his full powers, particularly how to become invisible. Then you will have to call to him by name inside your head. You'll soon hear his breathing when he is standing next to you for the first time."

Merrydown paused for a moment to catch his breath, then remembered his father's caution.

"That is no time to show that you are frightened. Simply hold your arm out straight at the side, and he will loop his neck down under it. Then, and only then can you truly say that you have fully bonded with your dragon. And remember, always, that only *if* he wants you to ride upon his back, he will show you how to do that, and whereabouts the special saddles are hidden."

Merrydown continued up the hill, feeling excited about the prospect of riding a real dragon, and yet somewhat cautious, with his father's words of warning remaining foremost in his mind.

"A dragon flying is something that no-one has seen for such a long time. So be careful to remain invisible. I will be allowed to see you both together, when you return home, for that is something which is reserved as a special privilege for Dragon-Masters only. No ordinary person may ever see that. Off you go now. Remember to be alert, and be safe."

"Why safe?" he wondered. "Surely once I am with '*Son-of- Fire*', nothing bad can befall me."

Merrydown's journey was uneventful, and after the steep climb he was at last standing at the mouth of the cave, a little out of breath, but eager to find the twinkling 'stone' that held his very own Shardlet, and see it become a real live dragon.

He felt inside his jacket to ensure that the dragon's tooth knife was easily accessible, and then decided it would be better if he placed it in the waist-band of his trousers. With one last look behind him, he stepped into the darkness within the tunnel.

He was absolutely certain that no-one had followed him, but, just to make certain, he turned around and carefully peered out of the tunnel once more, whilst ensuring that he could not be seen from that vantage point.

There was no-one to be seen, and so, happy to continue with his quest, Merrydown felt his way through the darkness very carefully.

As he inched his way through the long winding tunnel that led from the cave-mouth into the body of the cave itself, he began to see that strange glow once again from the Shardlets.

The glow gradually changed into the now familiar twinkling from the Shardlets scattered all around the cave floor.

He tried to distinguish the one his father had replaced back on the cave floor after it had been restored to a complete 'stone' again, from their previous visit. But there were just so many to choose from that Merrydown was starting to feel quite dismayed.

He thought that it was going to be an almost impossible task after all, and was now beginning to wish that Gavin had come with him.

But then he felt the knife at his side starting to pulsate, and so he removed it from his waistband to see why. As he did so, he could feel it pulling gently one particular way.

He turned to face that direction, whilst holding it out in front of him, and then Merrydown suddenly saw that one of the Shardlets had begun to glow more brightly than the others.

Was that the one he was seeking?

He bent down and picked it up. It tingled in his hand, and so he stood up, and very carefully drew the dragon's tooth knife across one end of the 'stone' just as his father had done.

It neatly fell into two uneven parts, and the Shardlet slithered out into his hand, looking quite fierce for such a small thing. This time, it was also very much awake, and its little tail curled around and under its back legs.

At the same time, he heard gentle words beginning to form, in what could only be described as a whisper, but strangely, not in his ears.

Don't be alarmed, Merrydown. I felt you needed my help in finding which of the Shardlets was me, came the dragon's voice, somewhere deep inside his head.

Surely you were already aware that I had instantly formed a bond with you from the last time you held me in your hand, and therefore it only took a small effort on my part to shine even brighter than my brothers and sisters, to enable you to find me more easily.

Merrydown sensed the bond between them growing and strengthening with the Shardlet's words.

I am so pleased that you honoured my mother by naming me 'Son-of-Fire', and I am more than happy to help with whatever it is that has caused you to wake me from my long sleep. I believe that the two of us will become good friends. There is no need to use words when we communicate, he reminded Merrydown. *From now on, you only need to think something, I will hear you, and happily assist.*

The Shardlet sat quietly in Merrydown's hand with its tail curled around a back leg.

Chapter Eight

Spying on the Spy

Merrydown almost started to speak out loud, more out of habit than anything else, and then corrected himself. He found this a difficult process at first, and it felt very strange indeed.

He struggled to form any thoughts clearly as it was a whole new experience for him. For the first time in his life, he now had to learn how to control what he thought, as he knew that someone – his Shardlet – could read his thoughts. It was initially quite unsettling.

Merrydown carefully explained to his Shardlet exactly what he was going to be asked to do, in the same way that the Shardlet had communicated with him, formulating the words silently in his mind.

"Our country is at war with Germany for a second time. Are you willing to help both my father Gavin, and I try and keep an eye on someone we know is an imposter, and who is likely to also be a spy for the enemy too?"

He felt, rather than heard the Shardlet's agreement through their bond.

"As I'm sure you know already, from reading my thoughts, I will need to take you out into the daylight so you can become a full-grown dragon, and then fully develop your powers. Once you have done so, you can become invisible and then secretly observe this man's comings and goings until the men from British Security can arrive from London and take over from us."

Merrydown made his way carefully out of the cave, this time, it was much easier to see his way, as simply holding Son-of-Fire in his outstretched hand in front of him, lit up his way through to almost the very mouth of the tunnel.

As they approached it, daylight could just be seen as a faint glow up ahead.

Son-of-Fire then whispered inside his head once again.

Merrydown, you will now need to carefully cup your hands around and over me until we get out into the full light of day, or I will become full-sized too quickly and may become stuck.

You see, a female dragon is much smaller than a male, but even so, she has to crawl on her stomach through this tunnel to get into the cave where she had made her nest and cared for her eggs.

Once you get fully into the daylight, you must throw your hands up in the air and well away from you as you release me, then stand as far back as you can until I have fully ceased to be visible, after which, I will come to back to you.

But first, just set me down here in the shadows and make sure that no-one is about outside. If we are at war, you cannot be too careful!

Merrydown did as he was bid, and returned after a few moments, smiling.

He picked up Son-of-Fire and wrapped his fingers carefully all around the little Shardlet, after tucking its tail well under with his thumbs.

Then he went to the mouth of the cave, took a further two steps, and threw up his hands whilst quickly releasing the Shardlet as instructed. He then stepped back immediately.

To his amazement, the Shardlet disappeared in a flash of violet light almost as bright as the sun, completely dazzling Merrydown for about two minutes.

When he could see again, there in front of him was a beautiful, full-sized white dragon. As he watched, something very weird was happening. The dragon was disappearing before his very eyes, and yet strangely, he could still see the faint outline of where the dragon really was.

You alone will always be able to know, or actually see, exactly where I am, said Son-of-Fire. *But no-one else will be able to see me whilst I am invisible.*

My invisibility, together with my armour-plated

scales are my main protection, you see, but I know by now that I am quite safe with you.

Then, a moment or two later, he felt the warmth of hot breath on the back of his neck. He lifted his left arm out to the side, placing his other hand against the cliff-face to steady himself.

He then felt a hard, scaly neck ease its way under his arm, almost lifting him on to his tip-toes in doing so.

It was at least twice as big as a shire-horse's head, and Merrydown now understood exactly why the dragon's tooth knife, now tucked safely back inside his jacket, was so big.

A beautiful white Dragon, *Son-of-Fire,* suddenly appeared, when Merrydown could at last see again.

Chapter Nine

Caught in the Act

"I'm anxious to get back home so I can introduce you to my father, as he has told me he is a Dragon-Master," thought Merrydown in his head, addressing the invisible dragon. "But it will be getting rather late for us to start watching this chap Richard Conman, unless we leave soon."

Don't you worry about that, replied Son-of-Fire. *I'll show you where our saddles have been hidden in an alcove on the far side of these cliffs and then you can safely ride on my back, protected all around you, and will also be invisible when I am.*

But first, to get there, you will have to hang on tightly with your arms locked around my neck so that you don't fall off. If you move forwards, you can jump up on my front right-hand side knee and then climb up as high as you can behind my head, and then hang on for dear life, for it will be a windy ride as it will be your first time. Now let's see what you are really made of, Merrydown!

Merrydown slowly walked forwards, and then could feel that Son-of-Fire had knelt down to allow him to scramble up his leg.

His dragon seemed huge, as he felt himself being lifted up into the air. He then shuffled up the invisible scales of its neck, with one leg either side, surprised that they were supple and not at all rough to the touch. When he was finally seated well behind the head, he heard the dragon think just one word quite loudly.

It was the first time that Merrydown had heard the dragon's inner voice raised. There must be something magic about the way it was used, he guessed.

Up!

They rose swiftly into the air but in what seemed like no time at all, they were soon swooping back down, to land outside what appeared to be a rock-fall, in a wooded area, hidden from view. His dragon become visible once again, and he nosed away a few of the larger rocks, to reveal a deep alcove in which were several large pieces of what looked like pieces of egg-shell, but all were shaped to just fit perfectly onto the shoulders of a dragon.

Son-of-Fire then carefully selected one of the seats and gave it to Merrydown. As soon as Merrydown wondered how to secure it, the shell appeared to magically attach to the dragon's scales.

Merrydown slid into the seat, amazed that it seemed to fit him perfectly. It surrounded him with the hard exterior that would both protect him, and, at the same time, also act as a windbreak when the dragon took off again.

Son-of-Fire nudged the rocks back into place, then as he took off, his horns, head, neck, and then gradually, the seat and Merrydown too, began to disappear. They were all still there, of course, because from where he was sitting, there was a faint outline still visible to show him where they were, but now they had become completely invisible to anyone else.

Merrydown giggled nervously as they flew higher and higher, but was calmed down almost immediately by the dragon asking him if all was well.

Once he had relaxed, Merrydown decided that this was much the best way to travel, now that he did not need to hang on for dear life.

They then flew towards the village intending to meet up with Gavin as soon as possible.

Merrydown was looking forward to commencing the watch on their target, using their new secret weapon, Son-of-Fire.

The dragon flew down from the cliffs, and hovered over the house and workshop, but as Gavin was talking to someone from the village about making a repair on the broken chair he was showing him, they landed in a clearing amongst some tall trees a little distance off, where Gavin usually got his logs from for their fire.

From there, they were well concealed from any prying eye, but to be on the safe side, the dragon remained invisible, whilst Merrydown was suddenly visible the moment he let go of the dragon, after clambering out of the seat and sliding off the dragons raised knee.

Merrydown waited at the edge of the trees until the villager left, and then walked quickly over to Gavin, who was just taking the broken chair into his workshop.

"Hello! We're back," said Merrydown as a greeting to his father. Gavin kept his voice low.

"Did you find the Shardlet? Did everything go without a hitch?" Merrydown nodded.

"You weren't as long as I thought, where is he then?"

"We landed in the middle of the trees," he replied. "Son-of-Fire is waiting to meet you."

"Lead on then, Son," said Gavin. "For if he is still invisible, I would never be able to find him."

*　　*　　*

Once they had locked up the workshop, they made their way into the woods, with Merrydown leading the way. He stopped in the clearing, and Gavin looked around expectantly.

Greetings, I am honoured to meet you, Dragon-

Master, I am Son-of-Fire, said the dragon, inside Gavin's head.

"And I am honoured to meet you, too." Gavin replied silently. "Hopefully Merrydown has explained why we have found it necessary to call upon you to help us, and by your presence here, I guess that you have agreed to help."

Gavin sensed Son-of-Fire's assent.

"It is quite like old times again, for it was necessary for my father to have the privilege of enlisting the aid of one of your family many years ago, during the First World War. His name was *'September'*, and before he and my father went to war, I was allowed to have a ride on him. I would consider it an honour, rather than a right, to see you, if you would reveal yourself to me."

With that, slowly, Gavin could make out the shimmering outline of the dragon, and when he was fully revealed, with his shining white scales, he could see just why the outline had given off that glow.

Son-of-Fire was simply the most beautiful creature Gavin had ever seen, and he was so proud to see both the dragon and his son Merrydown standing next to each other. He was filled with awe at the sight, and couldn't think of anything else to say. After a few moments, Gavin spoke, breaking the silence.

"Shall I take the first watch? I will wake you both in the morning, and you can watch him in the day-time."

Merrydown looked quite exhausted after the excitement of what he had been doing that day, and readily agreed with his father.

Merrydown said goodnight to the dragon, who became invisible again, before falling asleep in the centre of the clearing in the woods.

Then Merrydown headed home, while Gavin made his way down into the village inn, where he knew Mr Conman was staying.

Once there, he saw that the man was engrossed in a conversation with someone he had not seen before. He nodded a recognition to the locals on entering the bar area, and then sat down where he could see everything that was happening, and also he was able to overhear part of their conversation, too.

After being served with his usual pint of bitter, Gavin turned away from the barman to where Mr Conman and his friend were seated at the small table situated quite near the inn's log fire, which was getting rather low.

The barman, who knew Gavin very well, said that he needed another delivery of logs from Gavin, and then asked him to stick another log on the fire from the small stack adjacent to the hearth, while he served another customer.

Gavin was happy to oblige, as it would allow him to get a better look at the stranger that Mr Conman was talking with without drawing suspicion to himself.

Although the man was rather slim, Gavin noticed that there appeared to be a weapon concealed under his jacket.

As Gavin turned away from putting a log on the fire, he noticed other details of the man's appearance. He had very fair hair, cut quite short, and also the most blue, piercing eyes that Gavin had ever seen. His jacket was almost identical to the one Mr Conman was wearing. In fact, that, if nothing else, would ensure that they would be easy to spot, just as you would notice a pair of twins who wore the same clothes.

The stranger leaned over to Mr Conman and asked in a low voice who Gavin was, but not low enough, as Gavin heard him ask the question, as he was really straining to take in what had been asked.

"That's the carpenter chap I told you about in my report. You will remember that I had followed him and his son up to those caves before I met with my little mishap in the tunnel. He was very helpful in rendering first-aid, and brought me back down to the village after my little accident. I still think he could be the one to lead us to the lair of the dragons, if such rumours happen to be proved true."

"Ja," said the stranger in response. "You know that the Furher seems obsessed with the supernatural, mythology, and so on, so we must make sure that this thing really does exist. If so, it could be used as a powerful weapon. After all, it is on their flag. That cannot just be a coincidence. We will go up to those caves together tomorrow and have a really good look around without anyone finding out."

He leant back again in his chair, sure that he had not been overheard.

Gavin had guessed from the stranger's 'Ja' slip that he couldn't be anything other than a German, and his suspicions about Mr Conman were correct. Without any doubt, he was a spy, and he was working for Adolph Hitler, the German leader.

Gavin's old army captain had been concerned about why the imposter was in their tiny Welsh village, and also what had happened to the real Richard Conman. Gavin had kept it to himself that they were in fact searching for dragons.

As there was nothing more Gavin could learn from the rest of their small-talk, he finished his drink, and had a second pint whilst standing at the bar, having decided that he would watch and wait until the two plotters stood up to leave.

They did this a short while later, having agreed to meet up the next morning at 8.45am at the rear of the inn, as most of the villagers would have all have gone off to work by then, so the pair would be less likely to be observed wandering around.

The German left the bar first, and Gavin watched through the window to see him drive away in a battered old grey Morris car that had been parked outside.

Mr Conman then walked up to the barman and asked for his bedroom key as he was staying at the inn. When this had been handed over, he nodded to Gavin and said good-night to both of them. He then made his way upstairs to his room.

Gavin left a few minutes later, as there was no point in him staying any longer.

* * *

The next morning at seven o'clock, after Gavin had gently awakened Merrydown with a welcome cup of tea, he conveyed all that had had seen and heard, and more importantly gave him a full description of the German so that Merrydown would recognise him.

Merrydown then went out to the woods, where his dragon had been sleeping, and told him all the news.

And so, by 8.30am, boy and dragon were stationed just outside the village, with a clear view of the back of the inn, they settled down to wait for the arrival of the grey Morris car and its driver.

The pair were, of course, unable to be seen, thanks to magic of the invisibility that the dragon had cloaked them with.

They didn't have to wait for long, for sure enough, exactly on time, the Morris appeared from the side of the inn and slowed down enough to allow Mr Conman to jump from the shadow of the back door and into the rear door of the car, which had been flung open for him by someone else seated in the back.

Merrydown and the dragon both wondered, unsurprisingly, at the same time, how many more people there were working for the enemy, for the German with the fair hair could be seen very clearly through the windscreen driving the car. And there was someone else sitting next to him.

Merrydown wondered why Mr Conman and his companion also needed two more men to accompany them on a trip to the cliffs where the caves were hidden, but all was soon to be revealed.

The car drove off quickly and the village was soon left well behind, with Merrydown following high above them in his seat on the dragon's back, and all the while they remained quite invisible, and so the people in the car being driven by the German didn't have a clue that they were being followed.

The car continued along the road in the direction of the cliffs, but just a couple of miles from their destination, on the brow of a hill that was covered in tall bracken, the car came to a sudden stop. One of the passengers got out of the car and quickly secreted himself in the bracken, carrying what looked like a bulky back-pack with him.

Merrydown could see the man was now extending a thin telescopic radio mast from it. It was obvious now why he had been in the car. He was to act as a lookout, and warn the others if anyone was approaching the others, by using the radio that was in the back-pack.

The car then continued on its journey until the road could not take them any closer to the cliffs, but they were now less than half a mile from the base of the cliff. They then had to park it at the side of the road, but rather than leave it looking as though it had been abandoned, one man remained in the car.

Merrydown guessed that there must be a receiver in the car, in order that the look-out could communicate with his friends if anyone was around, and that was why there was the fourth man in the German's car. Obviously they had arranged their trip with meticulously precision, but had not allowed for the unseen, invisible watchers high above them.

Although there had been heavy rain overnight, it happened to be a clear morning, and so they could see that Mr Conman was leading the German, who was slipping and sliding on the still wet rocky path up the cliff.

Although Mr Conman must have thought it would be easy to find his way back up to the cave, he did appear to be having some problems remembering the route, and had to back-track down again a couple of times before shaking his head at the German man. He looked quite annoyed at this point, as his boots and trousers, were, like his colleagues, all covered in mud. Merrydown couldn't help laughing at their situation.

He pointed up to the highest point of the cliff where the cave was hidden, and was waving his arm about in several different directions. At each place he pointed at, Mr Conman shook his head, as he could see that each way was impassable, and the German got angrier and angrier.

It was clear that he did not want to give up the search, whilst Mr Conman seemed to think it was hopeless. It was clear to Merrydown from the way the German stomped back down to the car ahead of his companion, that he was far from happy! When the two of them joined the third man, they turned the car around and collected their look-out chap and headed back to the village.

Chapter Ten

What Do Dragons Eat?

Merrydown and Son-of-Fire followed at a distance, and watched as the German's car eventually stopped at the back of the inn, and Mr Conman got out. It then drove off and had soon left the village far behind.

It was now heading for the coast, and Merrydown wasn't quite sure whether he should continue following them, or head back home to report the hilarious happenings to Gavin.

But when he discussed this with his dragon, the decision was made for him, for the dragon suddenly let Merrydown know in no uncertain terms what he wanted to do.

I'm tired, and hungry too, said Son-of-Fire, *don't forget that I haven't eaten since you woke me from my long sleep. I must have food, or I will soon be unable to fly much further, let alone stay invisible. I think it will be best if we head back to the woods near your home as quickly as we can. Then you can tell Gavin what happened today, whilst I go and get some food.*

Merrydown had no choice but to agree with the dragon. After all, they were a team, and were also becoming fast friends. Working together was by far the best way for them both to achieve a closer bond between them.

Then a thought struck Merrydown out of the blue. He didn't mean his dragon to hear it, of course, but as it concerned his friend, it couldn't be avoided.

What on earth do dragons eat? Had Gavin told him about that? He just couldn't remember, but of course, the dragon knew exactly what he liked. And with its stomach already starting to rumble, he quickly listed his favourite foods.

Why, fish, naturally, that's why we always go to the sea to die. It is to repay the ocean's gifts of food for us. It is always teeming with all sorts of delicacies, so we never get bored with the same diet.

Anyway, eating cattle always made the farmers unhappy, and I am sure that you had heard that nonsense about us eating fair maidens. That was a ridiculous rumour that we never managed to dispel.

With that, the dragon turned around and took Merrydown back to the village, landing in the woods. Gavin and Merrydown discussed the day's events so that he could again telephone London to keep them advised as to what had transpired, but still avoiding letting anyone know that he had now enlisted the aid of a real live dragon. Perhaps they would think that Gavin was mad! Meanwhile, Son-of-Fire went off to catch his supper.

When Gavin had finished making detailed notes about the full description of the two new men who had joined Richard Conman's little enterprise, and also full details about the car – colour and type, and in particular its number plate, he also made a guess as to why they had left the village and driven towards the sea.

They were most likely going to rendezvous with a ship, in order to advise Conman's superiors how far they had got in their search.

They had specifically singled out Newcastle Emlyn as the most likely place to find any real dragons. Quite how they had come to this decision was a complete mystery to Gavin, because as far as he was aware, the history of his family and the dragons had never been recorded for anyone to find. It was only ever passed down orally through the generations.

When Gavin checked his pocket for change for the telephone, he didn't have the two pennies that were necessary to put in the coin-slot to make the call, and had to ask Merrydown to raid his money-box and let him have some change for the half crown coin he was offering, which he was happy to do. He knew that his letter-box coin holder was mainly filled with pennies, earned running errands when he was younger. He didn't have many silver coins, but quite a few threepenny-bits, and loads of pennies.

However, as he knew that money was always in short supply in the family, which is why everyone had to go to work, he refused the offered coin. It felt good to do something personal to help the war-effort.

Gavin then went down to the red telephone-box in the village and telephoned Captain Greaves in London again. He thought it best to keep the part about using the dragon to keep them under surveillance, or even its existence, completely out of his report.

He simply let them know about the steps that the spies had taken to avoid being surprised or discovered by anyone, whilst they were snooping around and also told them about the portable radio.

Captain Greaves guessed that it had only a short range, and that they therefore had to get as close to the sea as possible to give their report. Gavin confirmed the fact that there were so many hills around, and the Captain guessed that these would have caused them problems with transmission over a long a distance too.

Gavin also felt that the fake Richard Conman's friends weren't the sort that were likely to give up the search so easily, and made his views very clear to his friend when making the call to London.

The captain was delighted with the report, and

also pleased to hear that Gavin thought that the imposter would still be snooping around when the army team arrived in two days' time to observe covertly and then arrest them when they had enough proof.

Gavin and Merrydown were congratulated on how well they had followed the spies, and also kept an eye on the strangers without either being seen, or even raising their suspicions. Little did he ever know that they had been given additional help from the most magical of helpers.

When Merrydown went back to the woods and told Son-of-Fire how well he had done, and in particular how important the dragon's role had been, and still was, he simply said that he had been happy to serve his country.

That made Merrydown smile, for he hadn't realised that the dragon felt that way about his living near the village, and that he looked upon the cave as his real 'home'. He was beginning to be aware that the dragon had feelings of identity too, just like a human being.

That evening, after supper, Gavin took Merrydown to the inn, and treated him to a glass of shandy, made of half and half of both beer and lemonade. That was the first time his dad had ever bought him a proper drink. Until then, he'd only ever had soft drinks at parties, and Gavin had usually gone down to the inn on his own. Now he felt like a real grown-up.

It also gave Gavin an excuse to be in the bar once again without raising Mr Conman's suspicions, while he was being watched by Gavin.

That was just as well, for, exactly at 9.00pm, who should walk into the bar and go and join Mr Conman at the table where he was sitting, but the German chap.

He was soon deep in conversation with the spy, but unfortunately neither father nor son could make out what they were saying, for it was a busy night in the bar because there was a darts match taking place.

Chapter Eleven

Visitors from London

Richard Conman and the German continued their conversation for a short while, with several glances their way, and quite a lot of shaking of the spy's head, whilst Gavin and Merrydown appeared to be engrossed in the darts match. In reality, however, they were both straining to hear any part of what the pair were discussing, as it might be of some use to Captain Greaves.

Eventually, as the final match of darts was completed, with much cheering from the winning team, even the spies found it impossible to carry on their conversation in the bar of the inn any longer, and with a shrug of the German's shoulders, he stood up to leave.

Mr Conman also stood up, and almost clicked his heels together, but looking quickly around, recovered from this obvious tell-tale sign, then shot out his right hand and shook the German's offered hand instead.

He hoped his mistake had not been noticed by

anyone, but when the German left, Mr Conman sat down, trying to blend into the crowd that were in the bar. This too was a mistake, for everyone else was on their feet, congratulating the last team member's perfectly thrown darts had which made it a decisive win for the visiting team.

Realising that his presence did not fit in, he squeezed through the crowd to the bar and asked for his room key. Without looking round at Gavin and Merrydown, he went up to his room, obviously having decided to call it a night.

Gavin waited a few minutes until Merrydown had finished drinking his shandy, and the two of them waved goodnight to the barman and also left the inn.

It was quite dark on the way home, and Gavin just made polite conversation about the game of darts they had both watched, as he was quite concerned that they might be overheard. Merrydown guessed that the small-talk was to ensure that any real discussion would take place once they were indoors, although he was itching to tell Gavin what few words he had been able to make out from the conspirators conversation in between the noise in the bar.

Once safely at home however, Gavin asked what it was that appeared to have excited Merrydown so much, as he could see from his face that he was itching to tell Gavin exactly what he had overheard.

"It wasn't a boat they had driven to the coast to send a radio message to last night," he said. "It was for the other two to be picked up by a dingy and taken back on board the U-boat they had come from the day before. Just imagine their cheek to show up in British waters. They must be very sure of themselves to have gotten through the sea defences so easily."

Gavin had a different view about this, as he told Merrydown that everyone in the War Office appeared to be more concerned that the shores along the South coast were better defended by destroyers and more protected by coastal foot-patrols in case of an invasion, whilst the Welsh coast was not considered to be an obvious target for an enemy landing, as it was right over the other side of the British Isles from France and Germany.

The following day, Gavin reported the evening's events by telephone to Captain Greaves in London, and was very pleased to learn that a small group of four specialists in surveillance had been gathered together a day sooner than expected, and was already prepared for the long journey by road from London as soon as daylight permitted.

They would be travelling over to Wales in an army van that had been disguised as a baker's van, complete with lettering in both the Welsh and English and the name of a baker's from Aberystwyth painted on the sides.

Inside however, it was equipped with both

short-wave and long-wave listening devices, and more importantly, a separate part of the van fitted out with a secure holding area where the spies, once captured, could be securely held whilst they were conveyed back to London, and, once charged with espionage for the enemy and proved guilty, could end up in prison, or perhaps in the Tower of London!

Merrydown could hardly wait to tell Son-of-Fire all about this in the morning, when he visited his dragon in the woods.

The dragon was pleased to see Merrydown, and showed this by pressing his large head gently against Merrydown's forehead in a sort of greeting.

As soon as he had done this however, he recoiled in horror, when he smelled the dragon's breath, as it burped and breathed out right at the same time, and right in his face. It was ghastly!

Then he noticed that the dragon's scales were still wet, and its breath smelled of oily fish, and was now none too fresh either, so it was clear to Merrydown that the dragon must have become hungry again, and had gone off under cover of darkness to catch fish at the coast, and had returned before first light.

Merrydown realised that it had perhaps only arrived a short time before him, and was still digesting his breakfast. He wouldn't make the mistake of getting too close to the dragons mouth next time.

The dragon listened as Merrydown told him what was going on, and then the pair of them became invisible and once Merrydown was seated, they took flight. Today would be the last day that they were going to play at the spying game themselves, and they again settled down to keep watch on the real spies until the team from London arrived to take over.

The team made good time, as they were quickly waved through all the checkpoints along the route, arriving at Gavin's workshop, in the early afternoon.

From where Merrydown and his dragon were positioned, they saw the van drive up the lane, and after a short wait, flew back to the woods, where Merrydown left his dragon and walked down to the workshop.

He was introduced to the team leader and the others, who were all wearing civilian clothes in order to blend in, but Merrydown had nothing new to add to Gavin's previous report, as Mr Conman had remained at the inn all day.

* * *

While three of the team were dispersed to take up concealed positions a short distance from each of the exit routes from the village, Gavin excitedly closed up the workshop for the day, then chatting like old friends, he and Sergeant Miles, walked to the inn.

They hadn't too long to wait before Sergeant Miles noticed the grey Morris car, pull up outside the inn.

It drove around to the back of the inn, presumably to pick up Mr Conman.

Sergeant Miles thanked Gavin, then headed out to the baker's van to follow Mr Conman. It was obvious that as the weather had improved, they were going to attempt to locate the caves.

While he drank his pint, Gavin mused over how they had known where to look. He wondered if it was because at Merrydown's coming-of-age initiation into manhood a few weeks earlier, there had been a traditional effigy of a dragon made of straw and bound with string, supported on two long wooden poles, which Merrydown had been paraded under by Gavin, as he had been taken to meet the village elders after his ceremony.

Everyone in the village had then helped to untie and dismantle the straw dragon and it was taken to feed the cattle. Quite a reversal of roles in fact, with the cattle eating the dragon – although only straw –rather than the dragon eating the cattle!

This was a reference to the old folklore of the village which had, in times gone by, apparently been plagued by a real dragon, if such a thing was true. Only Gavin, of course, knew the real truth about dragons. And, of course, now Merrydown too. But it was important to both of them that they continued to keep that knowledge a secret.

But thanks to the village gossips, the information had been picked up by the Germans, who seemed to be interested in anything 'supernatural' that might help them defeat their enemy. They now hoped that perhaps Newcastle Emlyn was not only the actual village that had experienced a real dragon in the past, but it might even still have real dragons today.

For the present however, Gavin kept these views to himself.

Chapter Twelve

Returning Fire

Gavin was told that the men from London were specialists in the field of counter-espionage, and expert at catching spies in particular.

They were so well-hidden whilst carrying out their task that when Merrydown, who was seated on Son-of-Fire's back, tried to spot them, he couldn't see even one of them.

Whilst circling around however, he did spot the now familiar Morris car approaching from the village.

Merrydown watched the car arrive at the cliffs, then park, and as he circled lower, he saw several men emerging from the rear of the car.

They were all wearing camouflage jackets and trousers and also what were obviously German Army boots, and he recognised the two men he had previously seen. He was surprised to see that there were another two men with them as well. These two also carried machine guns, which were slung over one shoulder. Clearly, they were not carrying these for show, but alarmingly, looked as if they were prepared to use them as well. They also carried long ropes over their shoulders.

It was clear that the German was determined to make the long and treacherous climb up to the caves, in order to check them out for any evidence that they had been used as nesting-sites, or even as a hiding place by a real dragon.

All this action was also observed by the team from London, and when they arrived at the base of the cliffs, were all in position to stop them. They knew that no one should be taking a climbing party up those cliffs, as they overlooked the location of several coal-mines, and were thus a sensitive location from a security point of view.

The British soldiers waited until the Germans had commenced their climb before challenging them to drop their weapons and surrender, as they would then be at a disadvantage should they try and use them whilst holding on to the ropes

Nevertheless, it was inevitable that both machine gunners did try to do just that.

One slipped and fell off his rope, shooting wildly in the wrong direction, unfortunately shooting the other gunner in the process. He became entangled in his rope, and just dangled limply there, dropping his gun to the bottom of the cliff.

The other soldiers with them, who were still at the base of the cliff, attempted to fire on the British soldiers, but returning fire from two of the team soon took care of them, thankfully, without any loss from the British.

Their leader shot up his hands in surrender, and was quickly surrounded by the team, arrested, and eventually bundled into the baker's van, hand-cuffed and bound, and locked in the secure cage.

The other Germans who had died were placed into the rear of the van and the British soldiers also got into the back.

The van was then driven back to Gavin's workshop, where the Sergeant thanked Gavin for all his help.

Merrydown, meanwhile, had witnessed all of the action from his seat on the dragon's back, and only turned up in time to say goodbye when the team left for London, where the surviving German would be interrogated. The senior officer also thanked him too.

He said to Merrydown, "I'm sorry that you missed all the 'fireworks', but I guess that you were in a much safer place at the time. Just imagine, the Germans made all that effort, and lost four men too, in what turned out to be a futile search for dragons. Can you imagine, in this day and age, anyone believing in dragons?"

Merrydown smiled at Gavin, and the pair of them simply couldn't stop laughing as the baker's van drove away.

"I wish we could do more to help with the war-effort," said Merrydown, when they could speak again.

Gavin told Merrydown that he would think about that, but both of them had had quite enough excitement for one day. Gavin then suggested to Merrydown that his dragon might have a few ideas that could help too, and so Merrydown went off to the woods to talk to him about the matter.

Chapter Thirteen

Airborne again

"Son-of-Fire said that he would give the matter some great thought," said Merrydown to Gavin on his return later that day. "He said he had enjoyed his part in defending his country, and would be happy to do so again if called upon."

Gavin nodded and handed him a cup of tea.

"He also said that he would try to hunt down the German submarine whilst he was chasing fish to eat. But I put him off that idea as it would mean revealing himself, as there was no way that you could possibly have any knowledge about the whereabouts of a German U-Boat, if he had come across it."

Father and son settled onto the sofa and Merrydown continued.

"You couldn't report that to the British Navy, they would wonder how you had got that information, and it would have caused far too many questions."

"Very wise of you to have thought that all

through," said Gavin to his son. "It certainly shows how mature you have become now that you have accepted the responsibility for the safety of your dragon. I guess we had better sleep on it, and see what we all come up with in the morning."

"Before we go to bed, could you tell me a little more about grandfather's dragon, September?"

"It was just before the First World War," said Gavin. "And your grandfather was drafted into the army. He awoke his dragon, who went with him, to keep him safe. He was trained as a gunner, and during the war, was in position on top of a water-tank as he was guarding an airfield. His position was under heavy fire, and his dragon was keeping him advised of any danger, when an aeroplane flew straight into September from behind as he was invisible."

Merrydown's eyes widened, and he sipped the last of his tea.

"Sadly, both the pilot and September perished when the aeroplane exploded in a ball of fire. There was nothing that your grandfather could have done to warn him, because he was too high up to be seen. But after the fire died down, he found a lone dragon's tooth, which was all that remained. It was a terrible personal loss, for his dragon had saved his life on so many occasions before that terrible accident occurred."

Both were quiet for a little while after that revelation, out of respect for the lost dragon, and then Gavin leaned over to turn on the radio to listen to the news programme, and heard that the war in the air had not been going too well. In fact, some returning bombers had actually crashed into the cliffs at Dover because they were so badly damaged that they couldn't gain enough height to lift over them, causing a sad loss of air-crew and airplanes.

Gavin finally went to bed with the germ of an idea starting to form in his head. By the time he awoke the next morning, he had come up with what he thought was a great idea, and after waiting for Emmeline and her mother to go back to work at the farm once again, he explained his idea to Merrydown.

"I think that it's a great idea," said Merrydown, once Gavin had outlined where he had got the idea from and how he thought both Merrydown and Son-of-Fire could be instrumental in saving lives. Then he added, "But I think we should include my dragon in our discussions, before we go any further with this. I know that it is still quite early in the day, but let's go down to the woods right now and wake him up. I'm sure he has slept well after all that excitement yesterday."

And so the pair locked up the house and workshop, and Gavin picked up his large saw and an axe, so if anyone saw them going into the woods so often, it would just appear as if they were going to cut up another of the trees that they had felled the previous winter, and would now be seasoned enough to burn well when made into logs, or even be made into furniture. Green wood was no use for either. Merrydown took their wheelbarrow, and they walked into the clearing where the dragon was sleeping, but, as always, with one eye open.

And of course, for everyone's safety, he had remained invisible. This was because anyone who might have trespassed and gone into Gavin's woods to take some of his firewood – without paying for it – would have seen the dragon and raised the alarm, causing a panic. After all, it was war-time, and all things were in short supply, including wood for their home fires.

Merrydown woke the dragon properly with a greeting, and he then revealed himself to both father and son, which was a respectful thing to do as Gavin was also a Dragon-Master in his own right.

Gavin silently addressed Son-of-Fire. "Merrydown said that you would be interested in helping the war-effort again. I gave the matter a lot of thought after listening to the news on the radio last night, and I think there is a way to do that without endangering either you, or my son. You see, the British have lost air-crew and aeroplanes after they have been badly damaged in battle, and although they have successfully limped home across the sea, they then crash and perish against the high coastal cliffs because they cannot maintain enough lift."

Son-of-Fire nodded for Gavin to continue.

"I was thinking perhaps you could base yourself and Merrydown just outside Dover. Then when damaged planes return to British shores, you could secretly fly underneath them whilst invisible, and help to keep high enough for them to get over the top of the cliffs and then be able to safely land."

Son-of-Fire drew himself to his full height, accepting the suggestion as though it were a mission.

"What I don't want to happen is for either you or Merrydown to be put at any risk by going over to the Continent, so you must promise to stay within British coastal waters."

Merrydown and the dragon looked at each other and nodded.

"You can also help to tip some of the 'Doodle-bugs' over so they crash into the sea before reaching land." Son-of-Fire interrupted Gavin at this point with a question, shaking his head from side to side.

Just what are Doodle-bugs, I've never heard of such a thing before. Can I eat them?

"Oh no!" Gavin said with a smile. "They are massive rocket-propelled bombs, fired across the English Channel from France. When their engines cut out, they drop on unsuspecting people and homes and they are capable of blowing up rows of streets. London has been very badly hit with them. With your help, the pair of you would save countless lives."

Gavin noticed that Merrydown stood a little straighter at the prospect.

"Whilst speaking to Captain Greaves early this morning, as part of my now regular reporting, he told me that British military radio experts have tried stopping the rocket-bombs before they hit land, without too much success so far, so if you did what I have suggested, it would be something really positive that you can do. However, it is still quite a dangerous thing to undertake, so I would appreciate your thoughts about this idea."

Gavin and Merrydown waited for the dragon's response.

Son-of-Fire then spoke to both of them.

Merrydown, do you mind leaving home to do this? he asked. *From my point of view, I will not have as far to go to catch fish to eat, and a change of scene might be fun.*

"Of course," Gavin said. "Merrydown will have to travel quite a long way by train as turning up on a dragon's back would certainly give the game away. It's important that Aunt Gracie must just think he is visiting her, and his cousins."

Merrydown turned to his father, his face already glowing with excitement at the prospect of not only going on the train journey on his own for the first time, but also seeing his Aunt Gracie again.

And of course, he would be able to see both of his cousins too. It had been a couple of years since he had seen them all, as they were unable to travel to Wales for his coming-of-age celebrations due to Uncle Bill having been sadly killed along with many other sailors shortly after the war started, when his ship was torpedoed by a German U-Boat.

"I hope you can manage the workshop on your own while I am away," he said. "And it will be good fun to spend time with the twins. I can also tell Aunt Gracie personally how sorry I am about Uncle Bill, and take letters from Mum and Em too."

Gavin nodded, but before he could speak, Merrydown continued.

"I can take a food parcel to help out too. Oh! And I must make sure that I take my ration book with me as well, as I wouldn't want to miss out on my sweets."

Gavin laughed out loud at that point. "Well, you seem to have got it all worked out in your mind already, but we'll have to make up an excuse as to why it will just be you, and not your sister, who will be going.

"Em can go and visit them at some other time, perhaps once the war is over. It's anybody's guess how this war will turn out, and it may take even longer to get back to normal again than it did after the First World War, which was before you were born. It went on for four long years, and at the moment, nobody knows how long this one will drag on for."

Chapter Fourteen

White Cliffs of Dover

The day soon came when Mum, Em, and Gavin all saw Merrydown off at Aberystwyth train-station.

His old school satchel was being put to good use. In it were some cheese sandwiches for the journey, and a big bottle of pop with a stone stopper fitted with a rubber seal and a spring-clip to keep it from coming off and the lemonade going flat.

Also some jars of home-made jams, which was a real luxury and a jar of home-made mincemeat for Aunt Gracie to make tarts with. He also carried really long letters from his mum to her sister, and one from Emmeline to her cousin Tilly, who was the same age as her.

Tilly's twin, James, was to receive a new set of cricket-stumps and bales, which Gavin had made in the workshop himself, neatly tied up with previously saved brown paper and string. Everything in war-time was used on more than one occasion wherever possible, as it was necessary to be thrifty.

Already, everything was always in such short supply, and for that reason, many people were suffering because of the shortages. Pretty much everything was rationed, with points or coupons being distributed throughout the land, with a set limit for each person. If you wanted to buy almost anything at all, you were required to produce your ration book.

These ration books were stamped by the shop-keepers when anyone bought anything, and the mothers usually looked after the books, as they seemed to do most of the shopping.

These books allowed them to buy the rations weekly, but they still had to pay for the goods of course. If you did not produce them, then you wouldn't be able to buy even some of the usually basic foodstuffs that you could buy in peacetime.

It was war-time and items such as butter, eggs, sweets and sugar had become luxuries, even meat was rationed! And so a lot of people tried to buy what they needed from other sources, and there was a lot of money to be made if you had the right contacts. Buying from these sources was known as making purchases on the 'Black-Market'.

Wooden furniture was made to just a basic standard, and was stamped with a 'Utility Mark – (CC41) – so it could be inspected at the point of manufacture when built in a factory, because was in short supply.

Luckily however, Gavin's small workshop was exempt from this restriction, because he was able to cut his own timber from the woods he owned close to the house. He had sufficient customers from the village, which was growing until the start of the war, and even small repair jobs meant that money was coming in each week.

Merrydown's journey took quite a few hours, as he had to make a couple of changes and there were delays, but finally, he arrived at the station in Dover, where he should have been met by Aunt Gracie and the twins. They had been expecting him quite a bit earlier, but due to the delays, just James was waiting, as Aunt Gracie had gone home to prepare their supper.

James was delighted to receive the cricket-set Gavin had made, and was pretending to bowl at an imaginary batsman all the way to his house.

Once there, Merrydown handed over the other gifts and letters, and after Aunt Gracie had admired Gavin's handiwork, they all sat down to eat their evening meal.

Because it had been a late supper, it was now time for the twins to get ready for bed, as they had school the following day. Being a couple of years older, and not having school, Merrydown was able to go out for a walk on his own.

He was impatient to meet up with Son-of-Fire, as it had been almost twenty-four hours since he had seen his dragon, and he really missed him.

He had often played with James and Tilly when they were all younger, and the Dover Castle grounds were one of their favourite places to play, whilst the family had visited Dover on their holidays before the war had started.

Merrydown soon arrived there, having waved to the soldiers manning the searchlights and anti-aircraft guns, which protected that part of the coastline.

He was already aware of the dragon's presence, but couldn't make out exactly where he was, as of course, Son-of-Fire was invisible.

But then his nose caught a strong smell of fish quite near him, and a very strong feeling made him walk over to the nearest wall of the Castle. As he did so, there in the shadows he could again just make out the faint outline of the dragon's back.

Hello again, Merrydown, or should I say Dragon-Master, to give you your proper title? I'm so happy to see you have safely arrived, and I know that you had a long journey, as did I. Thankfully, mine was totally uneventful, I'm happy to report, and I have already had a very good feed.

The port here is very busy, so we will have to find somewhere far quieter for me to hide that isn't too far from your Aunt's house. I could sense when you had arrived at the station, and I followed you from way above, to see exactly where your Aunt's house was situated. Not too far away from the house there is a pretty big woodland area, which might suit us for our meeting up place. Hop on my back and we can go and have a look at it. You will find that your seat is already in place.

Merrydown walked into the darkness of the shadows by the Castle walls, and he quickly climbed up and settled himself comfortably into his seat, having become as invisible as his dragon was, from the moment he had first made contact with his scales.

One safely seated, the dragon and Merrydown rose gracefully and were soon high above the Castle. From there, in the twilight, he could clearly see all the way to the horizon, and was amazed to see how many ships were still in the harbour below, because the Germans had bombed Dover harbour in July of the previous year, 1940.

As soon as the dragon arrived above the woodland he had talked about, and before they tried to land, Merrydown looked down to his left, and could clearly see his Aunt's house way down below. It really was just a short walk across fields to the beginning of the trees, and then they both spotted the perfect clearing to land in.

Chapter Fifteen

Staying Out of Trouble

Once they landed, and Merrydown slid down the scales of his dragon, having made arrangements to meet up after breakfast, he bade goodnight to his friend.

The next day, the twins still had to attend their classes in the local school, as the term had not yet ended for the summer holidays. This gave Merrydown the freedom to continue with his 'holiday', and his aunt had made him a packed lunch of sorts – two apples and a fish-paste sandwich, which he packed into his old satchel. She did not expect him to be back until suppertime, and she was happy to refill his pop-bottle with very weak orange-squash to take with him as well. She was already looking after his ration book.

Merrydown said a polite 'Cheerio!' to his aunt and made his way back up to the trees behind his aunt's house, just a short walk through a few streets outside the town.

He then carefully made his way to where his friendly dragon was waiting, and once he had climbed aboard, they were soon invisible once again and flying way above the tops of the clouds, warmed by the morning sun.

The clouds soon burned off by the sun's rays, and they both had a clear view over the edge of the hills above the harbour, and way out to sea. In a short while, Merrydown's sharp eyes could make out a battered English bomber returning from an overnight raid, easily recognisable from the red, white and blue circles on its wings.

And hot on its tail were three German fighter planes, which Merrydown knew were Messerschmitt's, with their dark cross insignia clearly visible against the camouflage paint. But Merrydown's worried frown soon disappeared, when suddenly, a group of four Spitfires flew very low over the brow of the cliffs with a loud roar of their engines.

This startled both dragon and Merrydown, as they had not yet been that close to the airplanes before.

A 'dog-fight' followed out to sea, with the planes chasing, circling and swooping at terrifying speeds. The damaged bomber continued flying low and Merrydown watched with relief as it managed to find the extra thrust essential to lift it enough so that it managed to fly over the cliff-top, and it then headed on to its home airfield.

Meanwhile, the British and the German guns mounted on the fighter planes were chattering away and the paths of the bullets could clearly be seen from Merrydown's safe position high above the battle. Although it seemed to take forever, within a few minutes, and with spiralling smoke-trails, two of the German planes were downed by the daring and skill of the Spitfire pilots.

The pilot of one German plane ejected, and parachuted down through the expanding smoke-trails and landed in the sea. The other was not so lucky, and perished when the damaged plane exploded with a big flash, turning into a huge ball of flames. Burning debris was flying everywhere. It was a good job that both dragon – and his rider – were very high up, and yet they both felt the heat from the flames.

The third Messerschmitt turned tail at this point and fled back towards the French coast with the Spitfires in hot pursuit. The British planes followed it for quite a long way, but then turned and headed back to home shores, as it had become obvious to the flight leader that to follow it any further could be more dangerous, as there were sure to be more enemy planes and also the gun emplacements on the French side.

That was certainly exciting, said Son-of-Fire, in Merrydown's head. *I'm glad we stayed of the way, and didn't get caught up in the middle of all those guns firing all over the place. That would be foolish, and very dangerous too.*

I think we just stick to helping damaged bombers returning home, if they need an extra lift from below from my shoulders, or above using my claws, and we can see about the 'doodle-bugs' once we have had a look at one from a distance first. I'd much rather like to know exactly what we are up against, before we tackle one.

"I couldn't agree with you more. Let's head for home now, as I think that that was quite enough excitement for one day," responded Merrydown, and so they headed back to the clearing in the trees where they had met up that morning.

On the way back, Merrydown was in a very good mood, and felt it was the right thing to do to make up a song about his dragon, not really realising that he was following the tradition of his grandfather, and also his ancestor Dragon-Masters and Dragon-Riders. He simply felt that it was the right thing to do, and so, unusually, he not only thought it, but he also sang it out aloud to his dragon as well:

"Son-of Fire, you first took flight –
majestic – with your scales so white,
reflecting daylight, Oh! So bright,
Son-of-Fire – who fights for right.
Whilst safely seated, I can ride
across the skies, and also hide –
invisible when ere you choose,
and help fight battles we won't lose.

I know that war just isn't fun –
when there's a 'dog-fight' to be won.
And so I sing this song to you,
I never had a friend more true.

So fly my friend, and keep us safe –
out of harm's reach when guns strafe.
I'm glad we're on the winning side,
for nothing fills me with more pride."

You're too kind, Merrydown. I thank you for that moving tribute. Never forget though, that your safety is always going to be my primary concern.

Chapter Sixteen

Getting the Bug for 'Doodle-bugs'!

Once they had settled back amongst the trees, Merrydown found that after all that morning's excitement, he had developed quite an appetite, and so he thought it would be a good time to eat the packed lunch his Aunt had made for him.

As soon as he had unwrapped the fish-paste sandwich, his dragon, smelling the filling, licked his lips with his huge red tongue. His stomach made a very loud rumbling noise that almost sounded like thunder from where Merrydown was sitting, as he was leaning against his dragon's side to ensure that he still remained invisible, in case anyone might have walked through the trees and into the clearing where the pair were sitting.

Son-of-Fire then realised that he had missed breakfast himself, and hadn't eaten since the day before, and the smell of the fish-paste filling in the sandwich Merrydown was eating was so tempting, that he told Merrydown that he was going to go off to find a secluded cove where he could safely catch some fish for himself.

He said that Merrydown's offer to share his sandwich wouldn't have made even a tiny pin-prick in his appetite, so off he flew.

Merrydown sat himself down and leant against a large oak tree, facing the clearing. Once he had finished however, he dozed off, only to be woken by his dragon blowing his fishy breath all over Merrydown's face.

This trick showed Merrydown that his dragon, Son-of-Fire, certainly had a wicked sense of humour. Merrydown leapt up in surprise, rubbing his hands all over his face to try and wipe the strong fishy smell away, which was, of course, impossible.

Merrydown started laughing, and heard Son-of-Fire's chuckling in his mind. It was quite a while before they quietened down again. Merrydown was glad that he always had a handkerchief in his trouser pocket, and he used this to wipe his face and hands, but he could still smell fish for the rest of the day, only getting rid of it after he had used soap and hot water once he got back to his Aunt's house.

Over supper that same evening, Merrydown asked his Aunt to tell him more about the 'doodle-bugs'. The rockets were meant to cause as much damage as possible, and terrify the people into submission, just as the Japanese had done to the Chinese people in their own war.

All in all, this was a terrible decade for the world, and the prospects for the next decade didn't look very good either.

Far away on the other side of the world, the Japanese had already taken total control of almost all of Northern China, killing thousands in the process. War was a terrible business, and made people into monsters.

In Great Britain, people had already heard this terrible news, and were thankful that our Royal Air Force, (or RAF as it was commonly known), was trying their best to protect the country from the enemy.

In addition, Anti-Aircraft Guns (or Ack-Ack guns, to give them their nickname), fired upon the rockets with exploding shells, whilst they were being held in the spot-light by strong search-lights, shooting them down successfully on many occasions, but some did get through these defences.

Tipping or toppling the 'doodle-bugs' so they would crash, needed a pilot to bring his fighter alongside at the same speed as the rocket, and then lift the tip of the aeroplane's wing under the tail-fin, turning it over and forcing it to go down. These were very dangerous manoeuvres indeed, and it required considerable skill by the pilots, so only those with many hours flying experience were ever allowed to try to do this.

Merrydown discussed this information with

Son-of-Fire the next morning, and so they both agreed that they would watch how this was done by the skilled pilots first before attempting to do it for themselves.

Having watched the pilots over the next couple of days, they felt they understood the principle enough to try to have a go themselves, and try using both the fin-tip-flip method, where Son-of-Fire planned grab the fin in its claw and turn the rocket downwards. He also thought that his massive weight pressing down on top of the rocket and forcing it down-wards when flying at speed would also work.

Finally, only once they had studied both of these methods being practiced would they start to do their practice further out to sea than the aeroplanes went in order to intercept them.

This was in order not to be seen, and any that did get through their practice area would hopefully still be dealt with by the RAF fighters and the Ack-Ack guns.

Their first attempts were none too successful, but within a few tries, the dragon did manage to down one, by landing on top of it, and forcing it to tip its pointed nose downwards, and they followed it all the way down to where the very waves were.

They almost left it too late to break away, and turned upwards at the last moment. Merrydown could swear that he felt the sea-spray on his face. It was too close for comfort!

The 'doodle-bug' then plunged straight down into the sea, hitting in-between the swell of the tall waves below them, and it sank with a large splash.

Thankfully, it didn't explode, as it could have been deadly for both the dragon and his rider.

Unfortunately however, Son-of-Fire simply couldn't get the knack of grabbing the fin of the bomb in order to turn it, and that was because of another problem entirely.

This was not because of any lack of skill, but each time the dragon tried to do so, he seemed to slow down with the action of reaching out its claw to latch on to the fin.

In doing this, unfortunately there was increased wind-resistance, and no matter how they tried, they failed each time.

So they decided that they would just stick to the method of tipping the 'doodle-bug' downwards, but wouldn't get so close next time.

It's not as easy as we thought it would be, said Son-of-Fire. *And I must always keep you safe.*

Merrydown had no choice but to agree with the wisdom of the dragon.

Some 'doodle-bugs' still got through both dragon and RAF's defences however, but in much reduced numbers.

This was all very well during the daylight hours, and the dragon did manage to foil some of the rockets, but it would never have been possible to do this at night. And anyway, Merrydown's absence from his Aunt's home would be difficult to explain.

Their 'game' kept the pair pretty much well occupied each day for about a fortnight.

Once the next two weeks were over, the school summer holidays had started, but by then they had destroyed at least half a dozen more 'doodle-bugs' by themselves. Some of the rockets had managed to correct their flight despite being tipped, because they had a compensating gyroscope fitted to them, but as they were then already flying far too low, they hit and exploded against the white cliffs of Dover, causing a huge cloud of chalk and flint-stones to fly upwards.

Not a bad score, with many lives saved whilst doing their bit to help the war-effort, and not once had they been seen by anyone.

They both agreed that the time had come for the dragon to fly back home and wait in the cave in Wales, and Merrydown told him that he would join him in a few days' time, as he was obliged to spend some time with his cousins, as they were no longer at school.

He was quite sad to see Son-of-Fire go, but realised that as James was already planning outings for the next few days, it was necessary to go along with this, in order to keep his dragon very much a secret still.

Naturally, the next week flew by, with lots of fun chasing around the town of Dover with his cousins James and Tilly, and of course, wherever they went, their gas-masks always went with them, carried in a strong cardboard box, with a long string attached in a loop so it could be slung over their shoulders.

Too quickly, the time had come when they had to say their goodbyes.

During that week, they had even had to take cover a couple of times in the Anderson bomb-shelter at the end of the garden, and thought this great fun, oblivious to any real danger.

The shelters were not named after the Home Secretary, Sir John Anderson, as most people believed, but by a Dr David Anderson, an engineer who invented them to give ordinary people adequate protection from bombs. If their household annual income was below £250, they were given a shelter free of charge.

The shelter was usually placed over a deep hole dug in the garden. It was made of strong sheets of corrugated iron, bolted together, and it was covered over with a very thick layer of earth, in which some families even grew vegetables. It was so deep below ground level that they had to walk down four steps or more, and then duck down to go inside, keeping the door of the shelter safely shut behind them.

There was even a supply of clean water stored inside, and rough benches, plus some camp-beds. There was also a small table with a paraffin stove on it so they occupants could make tea and heat-up the tins of food that had been placed in a small cupboard by his Aunt, in case of such an emergency.

And so they could see, there was also a bicycle torch, and a hurricane lamp, plus some candles and a box of Swan Vestas matches as a standby source of light, because no-one ever knew how long they may have to stay in the shelter.

Everyone knew when to leave their houses and run to the shelters because the Air-Raid Warning sirens would sound the alarm, telling everyone to go and shelter somewhere safe. Those families who didn't have a shelter had to take cover under the kitchen table, or under a doorway, and hope for the best. Once the alert was over, a different alarm sounded the all-clear, and people would simply come out of hiding and get back to doing whatever it was they were doing before the alarm first went off.

The games were a great idea for a while, and the youngsters could forget the war for just a short while. But all good things must come to an end, and so eventually, it was time for Merrydown to make the long train journey back home to Wales once again.

Although he had only been away for three weeks, Merrydown was looking forward to seeing his family, and to telling Gavin all that had happened whilst he had been away. And what tales he had to tell too!

Most of all, he longed to see Son-of-Fire, because he had really missed him, and missed flying above the clouds, seated safely on his back. After all, just like his grandfather, he had now become an experienced Dragon-Rider himself!

Chapter Seventeen

Sudden Attack

The war continued on through to the next year, 1941, with no sign of stopping, and just before Christmas, more bad news came.

Whilst the Germans were trying to beat the British, at the same time, another war was still being waged by Japan against China, which had started a few years earlier. But this was so far from Europe that it had little effect on the general population of Great Britain.

Suddenly, and without any warning being given, on the 7th of December, 1941, the Japanese bombed the American fleet which was stationed at that time in Pearl Harbour, Hawaii.

Hundreds of soldiers and sailors were killed, and many ships were sunk, or extremely damaged and burning furiously. Also many civilians were killed or injured, and everyone was in a state of shock and horror.

As he told people much later on, the Prime Minister at the time, Mr Winston Churchill, said that this was the point at which he knew that the Germans would be defeated, and Britain would win the war.

This was because the unprecedented attack ensured that the Americans would now have no option but to join up with the Allied Forces, and together they would beat the Germans and the Japanese, who had joined forces with Hitler.

The next day, December 8th 1941, America and Great Britain jointly declared war on Japan. On the 12th of December 1941, Hungary and Romania declared war on America and the same day, India also declared war on Japan.

But it would still take a few more years before the Germans surrendered, and the Japanese did likewise, but no one knew that at the time, and they just did the best they could with all the food shortages, and the constant threat of bombs.

Most people had got used to the 'make-do and mend' idea, and children got used to wearing 'hand-me-downs' from older siblings. New clothes were a rarity, as coupons and points were saved to be used when someone grew up enough to start work, and then they would buy a new pair of trousers and a jumper or jacket.

At best, all that they could do, was to hope that the war did not take as long as the First World War had taken.

News coming from London through the regular contact Gavin made by telephoning Captain

Greaves was not good, as many of the air-raids had left bomb-sites in most streets in East London, and even an Army hospital as far away as Bournemouth had been bombed.

None of these awful bits of news had done anything to dampen the morale of the British population, who stood firm behind the Government of the day.

Both Merrydown and Gavin were kept busy in their workshop and there was little time for him to interact with his dragon during the day.

But each evening they would meet up in the woods and Son-of Fire would tell Merrydown what he had been doing through the daylight hours.

Despite Merrydown's protests, he had been flying like the wind at first light back to the Dover, where he was continuing to assist the airmen in damaged planes, tipping the 'doodle-bugs'.

I assisted one of our damaged planes in gaining enough height to fly over the top of the cliffs. It sustained enough power to get all the way back to its home airfield, but they never ever saw me, and must have thought they had miraculously got back 'on a wing and a prayer'.

Sometimes though, there was nothing to tell Merrydown at all, as the day was eventless.

But, on a busy day, the dragon was very happy to tell his friend:

Today, I'm pleased to tell you that two 'doodle-

bugs' were destroyed by lunchtime, but all quiet this afternoon, so I came back home as it was getting dark, it was hard to see anything in the poor light. But of course, I still managed to do a spot of fishing before I left the coast.

That much was obvious to Merrydown from his dragon's smelly breath.

Merrydown always worried about his friend, and so he often waited up for him until he had at last seen his dragon, before he finally went off to bed feeling quite exhausted almost every night. This was because repairing buildings with Gavin was very hard physical work, and often there was also quite a lot of travelling involved.

He was building up quite a rapport with his dragon, and on a couple of occasions it would take him on a night-flight when the weather permitted.

Merrydown was guessing quite accurately just where his dragon would be flying invisibly through intuition by now, simply by looking at his old school map that he kept by his bed just for that purpose.

He would then check with him later, and was amazed to learn how often he had guessed correctly exactly where his friend was, at a particular part of the coast earlier that same day.

The bonds between Merrydown and his dragon were getting stronger every day, which really pleased the pair of them.

Merrydown was told by his dragon that very

soon, all he needed to do was to call upon him mentally, using just his power of thoughts alone, and his dragon would know that he was needed, and quickly come to find him.

After a short time however, they eventually agreed that this power would only be used in an emergency, as to begin with, sometimes Merrydown had just called him when all he wanted was some company, and the dragon would be in the middle of catching his dinner, or doing something even more important.

Chapter Eighteen

Where is Son-of-Fire?

As it was still war-time, it was inevitable that one day something could go wrong.

Whilst eating his lunch of bread and cheese with Gavin one day, all mental contact with his dragon suddenly stopped.

This often happened when the dragon was under-water fishing for his supper, but that only happened for a short time, and was usually after dark. But this had never happened during the daytime.

He worried about Son-of-Fire for the rest of the day, and so did Gavin, when his son told him what had happened.

Later, once they were home again, he went out to the woods, hoping to find his dragon was there, but there was nothing but silence amongst the trees.

Merrydown waited in vain for over an hour. It had already become quite dark in the woods, and in a short while he began to feel rather cold.

Ghostly fingers of mist from a nearby stream were threading their way amongst the trees, and as each swirling wraith could be seen from the corner of his eye, he thought to himself that surely it was his dragon returning.

Each time he looked directly at the plume of mist, it dissipated into nothingness, and disappointed, he eventually gave up waiting and began to make his way home.

On his route home, he stopped to gather up small broken bits of branches to take home for the fire, as he knew that this would be a good cover for the inevitable questions from either his mum or Em as to why he was wandering around in the dark.

Gavin saw the look on his face as he dumped the bits of wood by the back door, and knew better than to ask.

After breakfast, when the two of them were alone, he nudged Merrydown gently in the ribs as he was putting the plates away in the cupboard and said: "Any thoughts on where our mutual friend has got to?"

Gavin was always careful never to use the word 'dragon' in case anyone might overhear him.

Merrydown shook his head. He hadn't an inkling as to what may have occurred to cause his dragon to be delayed, but he feared the worst.

Another day passed and there was still no sign of Son-of-Fire, but on the third day, Merrydown had a strong urge to go and visit the cave where he had first encountered his dragon whilst it was still just a Shardlet.

Gavin said if he felt that strongly about it, he should go to the cave. He even offered to go with Merrydown, but his son knew how busy his dad was, and was relieved that he could spare him for the next day.

Gavin woke his son up well before the girls were awake, and Merrydown was able to leave the house unseen, just as dawn was breaking.

Halfway there, he had already eaten the sandwich Gavin had kindly made for him, as he had not waited for breakfast, and as the early morning mist had not yet disappeared, he was very glad to have taken a flask of tea with him too, as it was quite a cloudy and chilly day.

By midday he had reached the cave mouth, and was making his way carefully through the tunnel towards the central cave itself, when he noticed what appeared to be fresh falls of rubble on the tunnel floor. Surely there had certainly not been anything like as many boulders strewn about on his previous visit.

Then he remembered that the Shardlet had told him that although a female dragon was not as large as a male one and would have no difficulty in getting back through the tunnel into the cave once she had become a fully grown dragon, a male dragon would find it a very tight squeeze to do the same.

Did that mean that his dragon had actually come home after all?

Had he managed to squeeze through the tunnel after all, dislodging the new boulders in the process?

Was he now hiding somewhere within the cave?

Merrydown was about to find out, but sensibly waited to call out to his dragon until he was standing in the centre of the cave, amongst the twinkling Shardlets.

He couldn't make out any dragon shapes in the low level of light, and so he then called out gently, "Are you there?" He was surprised to hear that his voice was wavering.

At the same time, he was trying hard to fight back the tears that had started to trickle down his face.

"Oh! Is that really you?"

What he heard in his head at long last, was a very weak reply from his dragon.

I'm so glad you came to see me.

His voice sounded a bit stronger now, and he slowly went on to tell Merrydown what had happened, and just why he was in such a poorly state.

He was no longer the shining white dragon he remembered from only a short time ago. He was battered and grimy, and had suffered a lot of badly scraped scales, and these looked very sore indeed.

Merrydown felt very sorry to see him like that. He then explained what had befallen him once he had flown back to Wales.

After a day in Dover, I made my way back west safely, and was busy fishing for supper near Aberystwyth, when I came across a German U-Boat. I was having a good look at it, and must have stayed with it for too long.

Suddenly, without any warning, it came under attack by a British destroyer which dropped depth-charges, successfully sinking the U-Boat.

I was too close, and was battered by the shockwaves. Luckily, I managed to get to a cove, before passing out.

Somehow, I got back to this cave, but in my battered state I knocked quite a lot more rocks off the walls and ceiling of the tunnel, causing quite a number of my scales to become more severely damaged, and my leg too.

I have been sleeping in one of the large alcoves at the side of the cave whilst I was healing myself, and as I was surrounded by the thickness of the rock of the cave, I couldn't get any messages through to you until last night, but even then, I was still very weak. I guess they weren't strong enough to reach you clearly.

All I could manage was to make you aware of where I was, but without any conversation of sorts taking place. I'm sorry if I worried you, but I'm feeling a lot better for seeing you at last, my dear friend.

The dragon then dragged himself out of the alcove, and Merrydown was shocked to see how badly injured his dragon really was. However, he managed to quickly wipe his tears of relief away, and then gently hugged Son-of-Fire's neck.

The dragon knew from that simple gesture, that Merrydown really had come to love him.

Chapter Nineteen

Life Must Go On

Merrydown asked Son-of-Fire if there was anything he could do to help his dragon to get better, but was assured that all his dragon needed to do was to remain in the cave and get a lot of sleep.

He told Merrydown that whilst he slept, he was able to heal himself, since he had enlisted the aid of the healing power of all the Shardlets in the cave, and they were all very happy to help him.

He had called upon them to help him when he had arrived back at the cave. His injuries had shocked the young Shardlets, who only knew about life in the cave.

The pair spent a long time 'chatting' about nothing in particular, but all too soon, the time had arrived for Merrydown to take his leave of the dragon for the time being, and return home to give Gavin the news.

In the end, both Merrydown and dragon decided that they would prefer to leave the fighting to the experts in future, and it was at this point that he let his dragon into a secret.

Merrydown then told his dragon that it was he himself who would be becoming an expert, as he had received his 'call-up' papers and was going to join the Royal Air Force. He then laughingly told him that he hoped that he was going to be trained to become a pilot, which had amused both of them.

It certainly cheered Gavin up a lot to see that his son was happy once again, and he was very relieved to hear that at least Son-of-Fire was still alive, although still recovering from his injuries.

For everyone concerned, World War II still carried on without any sign of peace in sight, and before anyone realised it, Merrydown had already turned eighteen, and very shortly was expected to join his unit for flying training.

He was fortunate that his flying training was not due to start until a week after his sister Emmeline's sixteenth birthday.

And so, he was able to remain in the village for her 'coming-of-age' celebrations.

Arrangements for this were already well in hand, and they were to be much the same as those that Merrydown had experienced a couple of years earlier, for the villagers would all be there on the day.

Emmeline was naturally very excited at the prospect, but she still hadn't a clue of what else awaited her on her sixteenth birthday. But secretly,

Merrydown had been busy rehearsing the words and history with Gavin to ensure he was word-perfect when he conducted the Ceremony and passed on to her the special knowledge that would make her, too, as involved with dragons as he and Gavin were.

For this time, it would be Merrydown who would be responsible for conducting the Ceremony in the cave for his sister to be initiated into the mysteries of her birth-right, and become a fully-fledged Dragon-Rider, because he, and not Gavin, was now the Guardian of the Dragon's Tooth knife.

And her initiation would be extra special, because it would also be in the presence of a full-sized and fully-healed dragon, Son-of-Fire!

But that, as they say, is another story….

About the Author

Always a traveller in time, space, and imagination, **Nala ha'Levi** has finally settled in Sussex, England, to realise his dream of becoming a writer, after the experiences of many lifetimes have now allowed him to be able to dedicate some personal time to himself.

He has lived not only on this planet – Earth – before, but on other planets too. Some so far away that they are impossible to locate, and on some that are now long dead, yet their signals are still audible in space; and on some that have yet to be discovered by man, in far-off galaxies.

It was on one of these distant worlds that he first encountered stories about dragons, and he has spent many years searching for the truth about them since discovering that they were also part of folklore in many cultures over our home planet.

He is a 'Wordsmith and Performance Poet' and has previously illustrated and published an Anthology titled 'Just *Imagine…'*
He also produces all the illustrations for his books.

56189375R00091

Made in the USA
Charleston, SC
14 May 2016